The Love Song of J. Edgar Hoover

Kinky Friedman

The Love Song of J. Edgar Hoover

WHEELER
PUBLISHING, INC.
ROCKLAND, MA

★ AN AMERICAN COMPANY ★

Published in Large Print by arrangement with
Simon & Schuster
in the United States and Canada.

Wheeler Large Print Book Series.

Set in 16 pt. Plantin.

Library of Congress Cataloging-in-Publication Data

Friedman, Kinky
    The love song of J. Edgar Hoover / Kinky Friedman.
       p. cm. — (Wheeler large print book series)
    ISBN 1-56895-394-1
    1. Large type books. 2. Private investigators—Fiction.
I. Title. II. Series
[PS3556.R527L68 1996b]
813'.54—dc21
                                     96-45016
                                        CIP

For Nelson Mandela
And the Eskimos
At the Airport

The Love Song
of J. Edgar Hoover

Chapter One

It was new Year's Day. I stood at the kitchen window sipping a hot, bitter espresso and gazing down at the raw, grainy, half-deserted, fog-shrouded countenance of Vandam Street. It looked a lot like I felt. On this day in 1953 Hank Williams had died somewhere along the way to a show in Canton, Ohio. Whether death is indeed preferable to doing a show in Canton, Ohio, has been a much disputed philosophical question ever since. About the only thing I could say for sure was that Hank Williams had been dead almost as long as I'd been alive, and the older I got the more he seemed to be catching up with me.

The cat sat smugly on the windowsill, smiling at a pigeon on the other side of the glass.

"You're probably a big fan of Hank Williams Jr.," I said, on a thinly disguised note of facetiousness.

The cat said nothing. She looked at me calmly for a moment, blinked several times, then returned her gaze to the pigeon.

I drank some more espresso and watched the fog. Facetiousness, I reflected, was one of many elements of subtlety that was most assuredly lost upon cats. It was also, of course, lost upon Hank Williams Jr. But that wasn't entirely his fault.

"How would you feel," I said to the cat, "if after every show somebody'd come backstage and said: 'You were good—but you'll *never* be as good as your *daddy?*'"

The cat continued to watch the pigeon. I continued to sip my espresso. The fog continued to roll across Vandam Street until it almost seemed to take on the bleak, beckoning, ghostly visage of

1

an early-fifties Tennessee highway heading inexorably toward the Canton, Ohio, of the mind.

I was contemplating the rather ludicrous notion of a man-and-cat suicide pact when the phones rang. There are two phones in the loft, on opposite sides of my desk. Both of them are red and both of them are connected to the same line in order to enhance the importance of any incoming wounded I may receive. Neither of them had rung in my recent memory. I walked across the kitchen and over to the desk and picked up the blower on the left.

"Start talkin'," I said.

"My name is Polly Price," said a husky voice. It was a woman I didn't know. As I reached inside the porcelain head of Sherlock Holmes for a cigar, I tried to think of a woman I could really say I did know.

"Polly want a private investigator?" I said hopefully.

"As a matter of fact," she said, "I do."

To calm the wild beating of my heart, I lopped the butt off the cigar and lit it with a kitchen match, always keeping the level of the flame slightly below the tip of the cigar. In my narrow experience as a country singer turned amateur detective, I'd had very few real live, honest-to-God, walk-in-off-the-streets clients. One of the reasons for this was that it was impossible to walk in off the street through the locked front doors of the building to get to my fourth-floor loft unless you stood out on the sidewalk and hollered loud enough to get my attention, whereupon I would toss you down the little black puppet head with the key wedged tightly into its friendly, ingenuous smile.

"Hello. Are you there?"

"Yes," I said. "How did you hear about us?" I glanced briefly at the cat. She had moved over to the kitchen table by now and seemed to be taking a bit more interest in the situation.

"I'd rather not discuss anything about the case over the *phone*," she said.

"Of course not," I said, puffing understandingly on the cigar. Woman was probably a little out of touch with the mother ship.

"I'd like to see you in person as soon as possible," she said, with a tone of urgency in her voice.

"Well, I have a very hectic schedule this week, but this sounds like a matter of some importance. Do you think you could be here within an hour?"

"Oh yes," said Polly Price gratefully. "And thank you, Mr. Friedman."

"Mucous garcias," I said.

I gave her the address and cradled the blower. Then I sat back in the chair and puffed peacefully on the cigar, blowing a thin blue stream of smoke toward the momentarily silent lesbian dance class in the loft above me. If Polly Price had the money, I thought, I had the time. The only other smudge on my docket was my friend McGovern's recent report that he was being followed by little green men or something to that effect. Why should I care if this mysterious woman was also being pursued by little green men? As long as her money was green.

"We've got a client!" I shouted, snapping out of my reverie, jumping up from the desk, and clapping my hands a few times to encourage the home team.

The cat, of course, was not overly fond of such sudden displays of adolescent enthusiasm. She jumped off the table and ran to the bedroom door-

3

way where she stopped and turned, thrashing her tail back and forth rather violently. She leveled an ancient, powerful green gaze in my direction, comprised in almost equal parts of distrust and disgust.

"Hold the weddin'," I said. "This client may turn out to be a gorgeous broad."

The cat did not seem remotely impressed. She turned and headed unmistakably in the direction of the litter box.

"Of course one never knows," I said. "Beauty's all in the eye of the beerholder."

Chapter Two

"If there's one thing I can't abide," I said to the cat, "it's a client who isn't punctual."

It was well over an hour later and the cat and I by now were back at the kitchen window staring glazedly into the street. The pigeon was long gone and I had no earthly idea what exactly the cat was gazing at. I had even less of an idea what I was gazing at. There was absolutely nothing in the street but a few parked garbage trucks and several residual wisps of fog that slowly eddied away like dreams from childhood or hopes from the sixties.

I was pacing back and forth across the dusty wooden living-room floor, cursing a woman who was not there, when I heard what sounded like the mating shriek of a pelican emanating from somewhere just inside my right earlobe. I walked over briskly to the window and at first I thought the fog was playing tricks on me.

Then I saw her. She was a tall, leggy blonde

dressed elegantly in black, and she seemed to be rising out of the fog like a pirate ship. I took the puppet head from the top of the refrigerator, opened the window, and tossed the little black head with the colorful parachute attached, down to her. Much to my chagrin, she let it bounce several times on the sidewalk before finally picking it up rather squeamishly. She looked at the smiling head but did not smile back at it. Then she looked up at me smiling down from the window. She did not smile back at me either.

"Fourth floor," I shouted, before closing the window. The cat looked on disapprovingly.

"Don't worry," I said. "When I've hooked a live one I know it."

A mere matter of moments later, the puppet head was residing comfortably back home on top of the refrigerator, the cat was residing comfortably on top of the desk, I was residing comfortably in my chair behind the desk, and Polly Price had parked her sleek torso in the nearby client's chair. She did not appear to be residing comfortably.

"You have been in Afghanistan, I perceive!" I said, as I lit a fresh cigar with a lox-colored Bic.

"You *are* good," she said. Her eyes widened eagerly and she leaned forward in her chair to reveal the ruthless outlines of a nice pair of zubers. "Just like I'd heard."

"I'm kind of semipsychic sometimes," I said. "Also, those are the first words Sherlock Holmes said when Dr. Stamford introduced him to Dr. Watson. 'You have been in Afghanistan, I perceive.'"

I leaned back in the chair and puffed pontifically on the cigar, studying my new potential client. I was enjoying my field of study.

"Of course, you realize," she said, "that Dr. Watson was no doubt wearing his Hard Rock Cafe/ Kabul T-shirt."

I chuckled warmly. She smiled for the first time, evidently savoring her own little joke. If this broad ever said anything really funny, she'd probably slay herself. On the other hand, there's always something especially nice about the first time a woman smiles at you. I contend that at that moment, if you observe her smile, her eyes, and her body language carefully, you can determine the nature and the depth of your future relationship with her.

"And now," she said, "I want you to help me find my husband."

Chapter Three

There are certain sacred moments in the oft-times jaded field of private investigation and this was decidedly one of them. It was the kind of thing you dreamed about when you were a kid. There is the mandatory moderately mysterious phone call. Then a mystical figure walks through the mist. A somber-spirited, beautiful woman dressed entirely in black enters your modest office carrying a little black puppet head with a big smile on its face. You take the puppet head from her pale hand and place it on top of the refrigerator. You glance at the puppet head, then you look in her eyes, then your gaze averts to the refrigerator. You are hungry, but only for truth. There is no need to open the refrigerator. You already know that the world is cold.

Now my new client is sitting across from me, fumbling in her purse for a cigarette, placing it nervously between her sulky lips. I reach across the cat to light her cigarette. The flame ignites. Our eyes meet again briefly and something is silently unlocked as if by an old-fashioned hotel key. She is ready.

"And now, Mrs. Price, before we find your husband we must find the answers to a few questions. First, how did you hear about me?"

"I was talking to a very nice young gentleman the other night. I was rather distraught, I'm afraid, and he seemed very kind and comforting. He recommended you highly."

"His name?"

"His name was Ratso."

I got up abruptly and walked over to the espresso machine to mask my disappointment and annoyance as well as my recognition of the name. It's always a bit of a letdown for a mender of destinies to suddenly find he's merely the butt of a puerile joke. Largely through my efforts, my semierstwhile friend Ratso had recently been able to locate his true birth mother and as a result now stood to inherit slightly under 57 million dollars. The matter was now in the courts, but the closer Ratso seemed to get to the family fortune the farther he seemed to keep his distance from his old friend the Kinkster. That was fine with me.

"Want an espresso?" I said curtly.

"That would be nice."

As if I were a part of the machinery itself, I robotically performed the standard prelaunch procedures for the espresso machine and kicked it into gear. It almost immediately started humming something that sounded vaguely like "The March of the Siamese Children."

"'Very nice young gentleman,' you say?" Some-

7

thing had to be wrong here. Ratso was many things but one of them was not a very nice young gentleman.

"Yes. Very clean-cut looking. Well dressed. Soft-spoken."

I thought about it for a moment. Something was definitely out of focus here. Even if Ratso had stood to inherit the World Bank, this transformation of style, grooming, and personality was impossible.

"Where did you meet this Ratso person?"

"In a bar."

"Well, at least that sounds right."

"He said he'd heard wonderful things about your reputation. He said you could probably find my husband much faster than the police without turning the whole thing into a carnival."

"My carnival left town a long time ago."

The espresso machine began hissing and steaming like a mad scientist's laboratory, so I drew a few cups and that seemed to settle it down a bit. Polly Price hadn't even told me her story and she'd already gotten her referral wrong. I took the two espressos over to the desk, set them between us, and fixed her with a stern gaze.

"You sure this guy wasn't ungroomed, unshaven, unkempt, and wearing antique red shoes, phlegm-colored trousers, and a coonskin cap with a little raccoon's head on the front with its eyes sewn shut?"

"Of course not," said my soon-to-be former client indignantly. "Who would go out in a ridiculous outfit like that?"

Ratso, I thought.

We'd been sipping espresso and staring at each other in sullen silence for several minutes before the solution to the Polly Price referral puzzle came to me. The whole matter was merely a case of mistaken identity.

"Where did you say this bar was where you met Ratso?"

"I didn't say," she responded coyly.

I stood up dramatically, walked over to the window, puffed purposefully with my back to her, sneering at the fog. After allowing the tension to build for a moment, I spun quickly around to face the woman in the chair.

"Why didn't you tell me," I said, with a slow, deliberate, deductive cadence to the words, "that the bar where you met this person was in Washington, D.C.?"

"My *God*," she said, not a little impressed, "you really *are* good."

"And now," I said, returning to my chair with her total confidence, "suppose you tell me about your husband."

Half an hour later, as twilight started to shadowbox with the city, I knew a little more about Derrick Price than I wanted to know. There'd been the standard private-investigator questions, the client's customary answers, the photograph of the missing husband, the tears, the proffered handkerchief, the plans to get together for an investigative lunch in the next day or two, and a cash retainer in an envelope, which I didn't count but which was too thick to slide under the door.

I didn't tell her, of course, that I was a two-Ratso man. There was New York Ratso and there was the infinitely more pleasant Washington Ratso, and as far as I knew, she was unaware that I was personally acquainted with either of them. As Sherlock himself had once said: "What you do in this world is a matter of no consequence; the question is what can you make people think you have done?"

As I watched the backs of her legs recede toward the door, I began to feel pretty good about the case. If I found her husband, it could really be a financial pleasure for the Kinkster. If I didn't, at least there would be a lot of opportunities to watch her legs. And there was a lot of leg to watch.

"One more question," I said, as she reached for the doorknob. She turned and again I noticed the pale, lovely face, the long blond hair, the blue eyes that came at you with the gentle ruthlessness of rain on the roof.

"*Have* you been in Afghanistan?" I said.

"Never."

"I suspected as much."

Chapter Four

Just as there's more than one way to find happiness in this world, or so I'm told, and there's more than one way to skin a cat, pardon the expression, there are also many different ways to conduct an investigation into the mysterious disappearance of the husband of a beautiful, long-legged blonde.

One of the most interesting ways is to get to know all you can about the missing husband by getting to know all you can about the client. This method is closely akin to the classic approach of Inspector Maigret, who, by the time he'd solved the case, had often practically fallen in love with the dead victim in his relentless efforts to get to know the nature of the killer.

Of course, my client was very much alive, and

her husband, for all I knew, might've gone out for cigarettes a week ago and then, without notifying the war department, decided to go to upstate New York to attend a hot-tub seminar on how to find his inner child. If that, indeed, were the scenario, my client would've found me so that I could go out and find her husband who was busy himself, of course, finding his inner child.

"We live in a world of missing persons," I said to the cat, as I poured a long, daunting shot of Jameson Irish whiskey into the old bull's horn.

The cat did not respond. She was sound asleep on the kitchen table, possibly dreaming she was in Afghanistan searching for her inner kitten. Judging from the peaceful expression on her face, however, it didn't appear as if she gave a damn about such matters. Maybe she was onto something.

I picked up the bull's horn, threw a silent toast to the puppet head, and killed the whole shot. It burned my throat all the way down like friendly fire, but it gave me a little buzz. One or two more like that, I thought, and I'd very likely be looking for myself.

As the cold fingers of darkness reached further into 199B Vandam Street, the cat made the short journey from the kitchen table to the desk, where she curled up under her private heat lamp and nodded out again. I found myself slowly pacing the floor of the drafty living room, a cigar in one hand and in the other the photograph of Derrick Price. I wasn't sure I could find him, and part of me, I must admit, almost didn't really want to. Maybe I'd seen too many movies like *The Maltese Falcon* or *Chinatown,* where the mysterious, grieving lady client winds up hosing the private investigator. Images of Polly Price came unbidden to my mind. As I paced, I realized that I was walking a fine line between the private side and the investigator side of my life.

I walked over to the counter and poured another Jameson into the bull's horn. Then I poured it down my neck. I'd meet Polly tomorrow, I figured. Learn everything there was to know about Derrick. All the secrets of their honeymoon. And soon, with any luck, he wouldn't be a missing person anymore. Like almost everybody else in the world, I was operating under the delusion that I had ethics.

"I'll find this bastard if it spoils my whole weekend," I said to the cat.

The cat moved not a hair. You know you're in trouble when you find yourself talking to a sleeping cat. There are far more tedious avenues of social intercourse, however. Like spending an evening with a deadly middle-class Jewish couple.

I was pondering the doorknob that Polly Price's pale hand had so recently twisted when the phones rang, making the cat and me both suddenly leap sideways. It was a slightly more traumatic experience for the cat, of course, who'd been sleeping on the middle of the desk in a position precisely equidistant from each red telephone.

"That's probably an important call," I said, wasting a little more facetiousness on the cat, who now was busy cleaning herself on the kitchen table, pretending for all the world that the phones were not ringing.

As things came to pass, it *was* an important call. Unfortunately, as you go through life, the things you think are important are very rarely important at all, and the things you think are not important are eventually, inexorably, vitally, profoundly, soulalteringly important. Then one day, like the wealthy British publishing magnate Robert Maxwell, you plunge off your yacht into the Mediterranean and drown yourself, saying only one last word: "Roseglub!"

I picked up the blower on the left.

"House of Pain," I said.

"Kinkster!" said the voice on the blower. "It's Peter Myers."

Cosmically enough, Peter Myers was a limey like Robert Maxwell, except that Pete Myers was alive and well and making quite a big success of his store, Myers of Keswick, on nearby Hudson Street. Myers specialized exclusively in gourmet British food, which, of course, is something of a contradiction in terms, thereby practically guaranteeing his continued good fortune in a place as perverse as New York. At the moment, however, Myers, who is usually cool and unflappable, sounded very highly agitato.

"Yes, Peter. Is anything the matter?"

"I'm afraid so. It's our large Irish friend McGovern."

"Ah, the Irish again. Where are you calling from, Peter?"

"The back of the shop."

"Where's McGovern?"

"The front of the shop."

"Well, that seems like a reasonable placement job. Will he stay there?"

"Will a tropical storm stay precisely on its coordinates, Kinkster? I don't bloody well know. I don't know how much grog he's had and I'm not a bloody shrink, but he's becoming increasingly belligerent and very paranoid. He thinks he's seeing little green men."

"They may not be little, Peter. They may not be green. They may not even be men. But if McGovern says he's seeing them, I can tell you that they're there."

"Well, I can tell you for sure one thing that they're *not*, Kinkster."

"What's that, Pete?"

"Customers."

I told Peter Myers I'd be right over and I cradled the blower. As my father often commented, this was *exactly* what I didn't want to happen. I was just getting ready to start searching for Derrick Price and up pops McGovern like a giant Irish jack-in-the-box. There was nothing I could do about it, however. You were stuck with your old friends. Like I've always said: You can pick your friends and you can pick your nose, but you can't wipe your friends off on your saddle.

I put on my coat and my cowboy hat, grabbed four cigars for the road, and headed for the door.

I left the cat in charge.

Chapter Five

As I headed up Hudson toward Myers of Keswick, a light rain began to fall into the night street, softening the lights of the city and lending the neon an almost comforting appearance, like cotton candy at a county fair. Refereeing a little tension convention between Pete Myers and Michael McGovern ought to be a simple matter for the Kinkster, I thought. I'd known Myers since before I'd realized how to correctly pronounce "Myers of Keswick." Pete, ever the well-mannered Brit, never bothered to correct my pronunciation.

But one day my friend Mick Brennan rather mockingly mentioned: "You'd think they'd teach you in Texas that the "w" in Keswick is silent, mate."

"Why don't you try to be," I'd told him.

I'd first met McGovern in a large closet—it would have to be—in my suite at the Essex House one night when I was doing *Saturday Night Live.* Both of us were flying on about eleven different kinds of herbs and spices at the time, so I can never be sure, but I believe the personage who gets the credit or the blame for introducing us was Piers Akerman, the world's smartest, and loudest, Australian. Why the three of us were in the closet at the same time is a matter of conjecture, but at least we eventually came out, which is more than many New Yorkers can say. When we emerged, I had a new, rather large Irish friend and I noticed that the suite was now full of other new friends, many of whom had Bob Marley falling out of their left nostrils and most of whom I've never seen again. At least I didn't have to waste any time trying to wipe them off on my saddle.

As the wind and rain turned colder, and Hudson Street conjoined Eighth Avenue, my thoughts, as well, turned to another subject: Polly Price. I could fill the New York Public Library with what I didn't know about the woman. What I did know was hardly enough to make for a good icebreaker at a cocktail party.

She'd been married for ten years to Derrick Price and, as with most successful marriages these days, they lived in separate cities, getting together only on weekends. He lived in New York. She lived in Washington, which, of course, was where she'd met Washington Ratso. And, as might be expected, both of them were lawyers. I don't know what the stats are, but marriages between lawyers seem to last longer than other unions, for some reason. Possibly the prospect of two lawyers snipping each other's legs off, then jousting in motorized wheelchairs during ugly, superlitigious divorce proceedings is enough to keep any marriage together.

Strangely enough, Polly Price had not seemed sure whether or not she suspected foul play. She seemed confused by the question. She definitely did not think that Derrick could be cheating. After watching the sensual way she smoked a cigarette, I didn't think he could be either. I was relieved not to be merely chasing some husband who was chasing a skirt that obviously did not belong to his wife. According to the *National Enquirer*, 98 percent of all those who suspect their spouses are cheating on them are correct. You can believe the *National Enquirer* or you can believe your spouse. Either one's a fairly long shot.

Only once during the initial interview had I asked Polly Price a really cold, surgical question. It was just after I'd lit her second cigarette and she'd crossed her legs for about the seventh time.

"Do you love your husband?" I'd said.

"Do you love your cat?" she'd replied.

It was a rather Talmudic and somewhat unsatisfactory response in many respects, but it did seem to demonstrate a slightly higher degree of perception in my client than I might've liked.

I legged it up Hudson past Jane Street and saw several limos parked out in front of 634, Myers of Keswick. I peered in the window of the shop and noticed a number of customers politely milling about and Pete standing nervously behind the counter. There was no sign of McGovern's mammoth form anywhere to be seen. So far, so good.

I loitered in the doorway and admiringly observed the operation Pete Myers had built through years of hard work. The clientele was, according to Peter, about 95 percent British and included everybody from royalty to the Rolling Stones. It was a loyal following that Myers of Keswick enjoyed, but it was also steeped stronger than Earl Grey tea in a sense of dignity and decorum. A guy like McGovern, if turned loose in a crowd like that, could send the whole business into the loo in a New York second.

"Where's Benny Hill!" came a loud roar from the back of the store. The customers looked around in embarrassed confusion. Pete Myers's face went white.

"Did you put him in the Dikstuffer?" came the roar again. The Dikstuffer was the actual trade name of a German sausage-making machine that Myers proudly had demonstrated for McGovern and myself in happier times. The machine forced sausage meat through a gleaming silver penislike projectile into the skin of the sausage. It was obvious from the perplexed expressions on the faces of the customers that they were unaware of the precise nature of the operation of this arcane device.

I walked through the hushed crowd just about the time Myers came flying around the counter, shaking his head and waving his arms, and we collided with an elderly Indian gentleman in a turban who was attempting to purchase four dozen curried chicken pies.

"You see what I mean, Kinkster!" said Myers in a voice of grim exasperation. "I don't want him out here with the customers. I can't get him to shut up. How do I get him out of the bloody shop?"

"It's going to take the entire Polish army or a forklift," I said, "to get McGovern to go anywhere he doesn't want to go. Of course, we could put him in the Dikstuffer." Myers did not find these suggestions humorous.

He peered cautiously through the doorway into the back of the store, as if it were the den of a particularly tedious dragon. "I love McGovern," said Myers. "He's one of my oldest friends."

"He's one of your biggest friends, too."

"We've been pissed together dozens of times but I've never seen him like this. I tell you, Kinkster, he's mad. I can see it in his eyes. He's bloody off the boil."

"What symptoms does the patient manifest? I mean, other than his recently expressed inquiry concerning Benny Hill and the Dikstuffer?"

"I'm not sure you grasp the seriousness of this," said Myers, grasping my shoulder like a drowning man. "This behavior didn't start this evening. It's been almost two weeks now! He saw a little green man. He believes he's being followed everywhere. He's getting phone calls in the middle of the night from people he claims are dead. He needs bloody professional help!"

"Okay. Settle down, Pete. You go back behind the counter and take care of your customers. I'll go back there and talk to McGovern."

It was a good plan, but it never really got off the blocks. McGovern came lumbering through the little doorway, knocking over a large display of the ubiquitous H.P. Sauce that every Englishman, for reasons unknown to the rest of the world, pours lavishly upon everything he eats. Several bottles smashed to the floor.

"Jolly old H.P. Sauce," shouted McGovern gleefully. "The British national drink! And you never have to taste the fucking food!"

"I say," said a nearby tweed-wrapped gentleman disapprovingly.

On his way to giving me a bear hug, McGovern managed to dislodge an entire wall that had formerly been constructed of cans of mushy peas, a gooey green substance much loved by the British.

"You know what's really in those cans?" said McGovern in a loud voice.

"Out!" shouted Myers, pointing his arm toward the front door.

"Let's go, mate," I said to McGovern in what I hoped was a Jiminy Cricket–like voice.

"See that old Indian guy," said McGovern in a hoarse whisper everyone in the store could hear.

"No, I can't see him, Mike."

"See that ol' bugger. The one with the receding turban—"

"'This is what comes of empire-building,'" I said, quoting *Breaker Morant* and aiming McGovern at the door.

"That old sod's been following me."

"Maybe he wants to know what's really inside those cans of mushy peas."

"It's *come* from the Jolly Green Giant," shouted McGovern, as he turned in the doorway and glared at the tableau of appalled patrons.

"I *say*," said the gentleman in the herringbone overcoat again.

"Didn't I meet you at the Boston Tea Party?" McGovern asked the man, as Myers flew around the counter again and the driver of one of the limos came over to help extricate this raging Irishman from the threshold of civilization.

"Who's this?" McGovern shouted. "A fucking footman from the royal coach? Come to fetch the princess some barley water for her gin?" I saw Myers wince slightly at this remark and realized that it had struck, apparently, very close to the truth.

After a somewhat unpleasant altercation with the limo driver, Myers and I were finally able to suck, fuck, and cajole the large, intransigent Irishman out of the little store, but not before McGovern had bombarded the few remaining customers with a rather extended series of "Cheerios!" and "Pip! Pip! Pip!s."

As I walked with McGovern away from Myers of Keswick, I gave Pete Myers a thumbs-up sign through the window. It was a gesture he did not return. He was already busy picking up cans of mushy peas.

"Where are we going now?" asked McGovern, with all the innocence of childhood.

"Well," I said, "I know a nice little French restaurant down the street."

Chapter Six

One of the most important aspects of human nature for an amateur private investigator, or even an amateur human being, to be aware of, was once, like almost everything else, quite adroitly put on a bumper sticker by Sherlock Holmes. "We are creatures of narrow habit," he said. For amateur private investigators or students of human nature, paying close heed to this observation can often facilitate your labors in the field and lead to remarkable results. As far as amateur human beings are concerned, there is almost nothing anyone can do or say that can serve to effectively guide us through the rabbit warren of life. This, possibly, is why so few of us ever turn pro.

McGovern, like most people, was a creature of narrow habit. When he drank he was out where the buses don't run and walking on his knuckles and the world had damn well better get out of his way. But, the vast majority of the time, when McGovern was sober, he was the rarest of human beings, a true gentleman. Tonight's little outburst had occurred when he had not been drinking. Something had happened that had caused him to go off the boil, as Myers had said, indeed, almost to the point of appearing to have undergone a personality transplant. I didn't know dick about art, but something was definitely wrong with this picture.

"It all started about two weeks ago," said McGovern, from the small, dark table in the back of the Corner Bistro, where I'd taken him for debriefing.

"What started? Whatever's going on, just tell me. I'll believe."

"Thank you, Peter Pan."

I'd plied McGovern with several Vodka McGoverns to return him to what I liked to think of as his normal state. For myself, I'd had several shots of Old Grand-Dad, to keep within bargepole distance of whatever wavelength he was on.

"Did I ever tell you about Leaning Jesus?"

"I think I would've remembered," I said, downing a medicinal portion of my third Old Grand-Dad.

"He was a guy I knew in Chicago almost forty years ago. Before I came to New York. I was just about sixteen when I first met him. I was working as a switchman for the railroads, and one night it was cold as hell and I went into a bar he owned on the South Side. He kind of took me under his wing. Let me drink in the place, taught me how to play gin, taught me a lot of other things. I was just a big kid. In fact, that's what he called me. The Kid."

"Well, you've certainly matured a great deal since then."

"He was an old man even at that time, it seemed. A very strange and interesting old man."

"'All right,' said the farmer's daughter to the traveling salesman, 'Why did they call him Leaning Jesus?'"

"Well, these old guys had a lot of colorful names for each other."

"Which guys?"

"I'm getting to that. Anyway, he was called Leaning Jesus because he was a thin, very biblical-looking guy with white hair who'd been in a bad automobile accident and broken his neck. He recovered eventually, but his head always leaned rather dramatically."

"To which side?"

"Left."

"Sorry, sir, but we've gotta cover every angle. We'll even try to cover *this*," I said, leaning over rather drastically myself, lifting one buttock, and expelling a highly audible fart into the candlelit atmosphere of young couples dining together at nearby tables.

I ordered another round for both of us to sort of settle things down a bit and then pressed ahead with the discussion, having no particular idea where the hell this was going. All I knew for sure was that I finally had a fat retainer sitting patiently back at the loft waiting for me to start looking for Polly Price's husband, and here I was listening to McGovern yap at great length about some character he'd known in Chicago almost forty years ago. If I'd only thought to put the retainer in the bank, by now it would probably have acquired some interest.

"Okay," I said, once the drinks had arrived, "what did this Leaning Jesus do?"

"What did he do?" said McGovern incredulously. "He taught me everything I needed to know as a kid growing up on the South Side of Chicago. He taught me how to live, how to gamble, how to hide, how to fence things, how to be an artful dodger."

"I understand that," I said, "but what did the guy do for a living besides owning a bar? I mean, did he have a day job?"

"I thought I told you that."

"If you did, I must have repressed it."

"He was Al Capone's chef," said McGovern.

"Leaning Jesus was Al Capone's chef?"

"Abso*loot*ely," said McGovern, in a pretty fair impersonation of one of the characters on *Amos 'n' Andy*.

"Jesus."

"No. *Leaning* Jesus."

I stared at McGovern for a moment, then stared at my drink, then raised my glass in a toast.

"To Leaning Jesus."

"To Leaning Jesus."

I believed McGovern implicitly. One of the things he never could be was a bullshitter. Besides, when you thought about it, Leaning Jesus was a perfect name for Al Capone's chef. He certainly wouldn't have been named Wolfgang Puck.

The other thing was that McGovern had known a lot of killers, murderers, and tough guys and dolls in his time laboring in the fields of the fifth estate. He'd done in-depth interviews with Richard Speck, Lieutenant Calley, and Charles Manson, to name just a few. Why shouldn't Leaning Jesus have been a perfect father figure for him?

"For the past two weeks," McGovern was saying, "my telephone and television have gone haywire. Ringing and turning on and off and fading in and out and electronic beeps all the time. And men watching me and following me everywhere I go—"

"Little green men?"

"One of them was," said McGovern defiantly.

I looked down at my drink again. This was worse than I'd thought. What was even sicker was that I found myself believing him.

"Look," I said, "don't worry about this now, bro. Don't even think about it. There's got to be a logical explanation for all this, and you can rest assured I'll find it."

"It all started with that phone call in the middle of the night about two weeks ago. That's when everything started fucking up."

"Don't worry about it. We'll get to the bottom of this."

McGovern now had a strange, dazed, faraway expression in his eyes that was not a particularly reassuring thing to see. I couldn't tell if he was drunk or sober, sane or crazier than Kafka.

"He was already a very old man when I left Chicago in sixty-seven. Yet, as God is my witness, he's the one who called me in the middle of the night two weeks ago."

"Who called you two weeks ago, McGovern?"

"Leaning Jesus, of course."

Chapter Seven

That night I couldn't sleep. McGovern had not been drinking before or during the Myers of Keswick incident, of that I was now certain. Therefore, I reflected, he clearly needed a major checkup from the neck up. Hearing from Leaning Jesus. Seeing a little green man. Of course, the mere fact that I'd found his ridiculous account almost credible might possibly indicate, I dimly realized, that I needed a checkup from the neck up as well. The more I lay in bed thinking about it, the crazier it all began to sound and the more convinced I became that these events had been occurring in one place and one place only—McGovern's large, well-oiled, life-marinated brain. Of course, there was another explanation for McGovern's bizarre experience, but, unpleasantly enough for all concerned, I didn't think of it at the time. If it had crossed my dusty, dream-laden desk, indeed, I probably would've dismissed the notion as more unbelievable than the one I was currently grappling with.

But McGovern's strange situation was only one of the Furies flying frenetically around my streetlamplit bedroom fending off Morpheus. Though I was probably the only Jew in America who never felt guilt, I began to half-see the distant specter of Polly Price's husband, his arms stretched out to me, his eyes imploring my help. Missing persons was always a bitch. Especially in those not uncommon instances in which the missing persons didn't want to be found.

I had a few missing persons in my own life, I thought, as I gently slid the cat off the pillow for the thirteenth time. She sulked a little while, walked around the bed a bit, and then came right back to the pillow. There has never been born a considerate cat. On the other hand, there are in this world very few truly considerate people. Considering that, it's a wonder anybody sleeps at all.

I missed people, both personally and professionally, I thought, as I lay wide awake listening to that great ceaseless buzzing energy that is New York at night. I would've liked to consult with Steve Rambam, who was the PI I'd most often worked with on previous cases. He'd no doubt have some ideas on how to start searching for Derrick Price. But Rambam was in Tel Aviv—or was it Rio this week, or Sri Lanka? Another missing person just when you needed him.

The other missing person was Stephanie DuPont, the gorgeous blonde who lived, and possibly loved, on the floor above me in dangerously close proximity to Winnie Katz's lesbian dance class. Stephanie had gone to St. Moritz with her family for their traditional holiday trip with all the other coochi-poochi-boomalini families of the world. Lots of missing persons there, no doubt. But I did miss Stephanie. She'd been invaluable in helping to find Ratso's mother, and she was the smartest, most attractive young person I'd ever met, and I had been having quite vivid, recurring dreams about her replacing the cat on my pillow.

Both Stephanie and Rambam were due back in the city within the next few weeks, but in the meantime I was going to have to show Polly Price something besides cigar smoke and two-way Ratso mirrors. For a while I thought about Polly Price, then I thought about her husband Derrick, then I thought about Polly again. Then I thought about replacing the cat with Polly on my pillow.

I still couldn't sleep.

I got up, made a cup of hot chocolate with marshmallows, and sipped it as I smoked a cigar in the semidark living room. People who've never had hot chocolate, marshmallows, and cigars together ought to give it a try. They say it helps you sleep.

When I got back to bed it was closing in on 4:00 a.m. and the cat lifted her head from the pillow and looked at me irritably. I lay back, stared at the ancient ceiling, and tried to make my mind a blank slate, but McGovern's large, somehow childlike, form kept spoiling my efforts. So I thought about Woody Hayes, the football coach, who was, of course, no relation to Ira Hayes, my personal hero. Ira, as you may know was the Pima Indian from Arizona who, along with five other men, raised the flag at Iwo Jima and appears in the famous picture taken after the battle. But that was another story, or was it a dream? At four o'clock in the morning whites and colors sometimes get mixed in your wash load.

Woody Hayes, I recalled, had once said in defense of his relentless ground game: "When you pass the football, three things can happen and two of them are bad." I applied this theorem to McGovern's current state of affairs and found that three things also could've been at work here. They were: alcohol, insanity, or he was telling the truth as he saw it. Unfortunately, of the three things that could've happened to create McGovern's bizarre situation, *all* of them were bad.

27

But lying awake at night wasn't entirely fruitless, I figured. Often you saw things you didn't see every day. There were a myriad of images, afterimages, dreams, almost-dreams, visions, and revisions that, like rare viruses in a rain forest, never would've survived the light. What was a mystery anyway, I wondered, but a shard, a tiny piece of the whole mosaic? And sometimes, through the infinite power of human imagination, this tiny piece falls into place.

"Everybody has the power of imagination," I said to the cat. "If we could only harness it."

The cat opened one jaundiced eye briefly, then closed it.

"Hell," I said, "imagination's bigger than the information superhighway."

The cat, evidently, had not heard of the information superhighway. So I explained it to her.

"You know the information superhighway," I said. "Where they spent twenty billion dollars so millions of people could wind up endlessly debating who was the better *Star Trek* captain?"

The cat said nothing. But then, she rarely if ever went in for pillow talk.

By the time dawn had begun flooding the city, cars were already crawling through the bridges and tunnels, people were already walking in the streets, and the cat and I were already sound asleep.

Chapter Eight

"Call me Polly."

"Okay, Polly."

It was early afternoon and we were seated at a table by the men's room in a crowded little Chi-

28

nese restaurant on Canal Street called Sun Sai Gai. Polly Price, looking earthier, more focused, but just as languorous and sultry as she had the evening before, was wanting to know if I'd had any ideas about how I planned to conduct the investigation. All I wanted to know was if they had any spare chopsticks lying around to prop open my eyes.

"I hadn't expected you to be burning the midnight oil quite so soon," she said.

"You can't start too soon," I said, "on a missing person case." I might as well let her think I'd been working on it. After all, she was letting me think she loved her husband.

"Today makes the fifth day Derrick's been missing?" I said, as the waiter brought a second pot of strong Chinese tea. Sometimes that's all that keeps you going.

"Yes," she said quietly.

"You know that I work fairly intuitively and in a rather unorthodox fashion. Sort of a country-and-western Miss Jane Marple approach."

Polly Price gave me a rather weak smile. I plodded on.

"That may well suit your needs, because, as I understand, you want this handled discreetly. It's always conceivable, no matter how well you thought you knew your husband, that he may indeed be a missing person by choice. He may have gotten in over his head on something. He was a partner, you say, with a very prestigious firm here in New York—"

"Schmeckel & Schmeckel," she said, matter-of-factly.

"Just consider the possibility," I said. "When someone in his position disappears without an apparent trace—which I haven't really determined yet—but if that's the case, things could get tedious. I'll need your help to start out on the right track. To do that, you may have to park your pride, park your ego, and park many of your previously held notions about your husband at the door."

I could feel her struggling with the idea. When she looked up at me there was the soft shine of sadness in her eyes.

"It's always hard to find parking in New York," I said.

In the next few minutes, as the food began to appear and then disappear from the table, we began to hammer out a basic approach to the puzzle of her husband's vanishing act. We'd go from the restaurant to her husband's penthouse on the Upper West Side, where she was currently staying. I would have free rein to go over his papers, his effects, his lodgings, his car, the viaticum of his life. She would begin assembling for me everything that would help me follow a paper trail to her husband. I explained to her that we might very well have to follow the trail backward before it would eventually lead us forward. She seemed to understand this, though I doubted if she was fully ready to accept its implications. It's always hard to believe that someone you've loved isn't the person you thought he was.

Or she was, I thought, as I daydreamed a little. I saw a girl in a peach-colored dress. She looked not a day older than when I'd first seen her as she drove up to the ranch in Texas in her white Thunderbird. She had a four-year-old son now. Lived in the Northwest. Working on her fourth or fifth husband, but who was counting? Geographically, culturally, philosophically undesirable, yet we were perfectly suited for each other in all the timeless, primitive, clandestine ways that can only be reckoned in daydreams. Maybe I'd take a trip some day.

"What were you *really* doing last night?" she was saying, as I felt my head give a slight, involuntary nod. She was smiling and waiting as I gathered whatever was left of my thoughts.

"It's an interesting, if somewhat tedious story," I said. "It mainly involves staying up half the night baby-sitting a crazy Irish poet who believes he's seeing little green men and getting phone calls from a dead mobster named Leaning Jesus."

"C'mon, Kinky," said Polly, laughing now for the first time that afternoon. "I don't believe there is such a person."

"As Leaning Jesus?"

"Well, him, too. But I'm thinking more of your journalist friend—just the image of you with your cowboy hat and cigar counseling someone who's obviously—"

"Cookin' on another planet?"

Polly Price was now laughing openly, whether from something I'd said or from hysteria, I couldn't tell. She had a wonderful, well-mannered, yet somehow wicked, way of putting her hand to her mouth when she laughed. It was a beautiful hand and a beautiful mouth. It was the kind of mouth you wanted to kiss even if you had to bite her fingers.

"When this is over," I said, "if you and I are still speaking, maybe I'll introduce you to McGovern."

"Great," she said. "If he's really cookin' on another planet, maybe we can share some recipes."

Now there were tears in her eyes. This was exactly what I didn't want to happen. A hysterical broad for a client, who'd recently misplaced her husband and was falling to pieces right in front of my eyes, along with the special added attraction of McGovern providing a nuisance nightmare of his own to occupy the spare time I almost certainly wasn't going to have. It was a hell of a way to ring in the new year.

I looked around and found a waiter and signaled to him to drop the hatchet. When I looked back at Polly Price, she was watching the people walking by the window with a dry-eyed, vacant gaze.

"Oh, Derrick," she said.

I paid the check and we got out of there. We found a taxi and headed uptown and over to the West Side.

Maybe she did love her husband.

Chapter Nine

Derrick Price's place was pretty swank and well ordered for a guy who wasn't home all that much. His penthouse, in a building with about nineteen doormen just off Riverside Drive, afforded a wraparound balcony upon which I was currently ensconced, sitting on some kind of modern, uncomfortable, wrought-iron chair, smoking a cigar and studying the view. New York was still there, all right. You just needed the Mount Palomar Observatory to see it. Polly was changing her clothes and I was changing my mind about how easy it was going to be to find the wealthy law partner who should've been sitting on this chair instead of me.

"Don't sit on that," said Polly, coming through

the sliding glass door in a slinky black outfit. "That's a piece of modern sculpture that Derrick made himself."

"Nice work," I said, getting up gingerly and rubbing my backside.

"Are you all right?"

"Well, I've bifurcated my buttocks rather severely, but it's probably not the last time I'll make an ass out of myself. Let's get cracking."

I told Polly what I felt I needed: her husband's date of birth and social security number, and any bank statements, phone bills, or credit-card billings or receipts that might provide a clue to his activities right before he disappeared. As she set about gathering these items, I poked around the apartment a bit on my own. There didn't seem to be anything out of place or just lying about. Polly had told me she'd touched very little and hadn't moved anything around in the place.

"Has the maid been in lately?" I asked, as I came into the room where Polly was excavating papers from a desk.

"Derrick doesn't have a maid." She was still hanging in there with the present tense, I noticed. I wondered how long that was going to last.

"Big place like this," I said. "You'd think he'd need twelve maids a milkin'."

"Derrick's very anal."

"All successful lawyers are very anal," I said. "That's part of their charm. I don't see a Christmas tree."

"Derrick's very secular."

"Okay, so he's very anal and he's very secular. What else is he?"

"A very good husband," she said, putting her head in her hands and beginning to stoke up the waterworks again. I let them flow. There was something she wasn't telling me, I thought. And that can often take an investigation from merely tedious to extremely unpleasant in a hurry.

I checked out the kitchen which looked like it'd never seen a cockroach. Of course, cockroaches had more brains than to go into a kitchen where there wasn't any food. I wandered into the living room and it, too, had the same unlived-in feel. Few personal effects. No photos of the happy couple anywhere on the tables or walls. It had the feel of a well-appointed boardroom or a suite in an upscale hotel. Maybe it wasn't that strange, I thought. Not everybody appreciated cats, dead cigars, a layer of dust on the floor, and a lesbian dance class on the ceiling as much as I did.

I looked in Derrick's bedroom, where Polly had been sleeping for the past few nights. She was fairly anal retentive herself, and everything was neat as a pin, including photos and bric-a-brac and personal effects all in such a symmetry as to make even the great Hercule Poirot twirl his mustache in satisfaction. But which of the photos and effects were Polly's and which were Derrick's wasn't readily discernible.

I took the picture of Derrick that Polly had given me and compared it with several on the bed table. He didn't look as happy in my shot. Of course, in my photo he wasn't with Polly. I tried to think of him, in Dickens's phrase, as a "fellow passenger to the grave." Derrick Price had been a man just like myself, I thought. His flight, very possibly, had just gotten in a little earlier.

If Fibber McGee had been gay he would've come out of Derrick Price's closet in a hurry. Every suit, every tie, every shoe was in its place. It looked almost like a store display. What a pathologically impeccable man Price was. How could he come to such an untidy end?

I sat on the bed and looked out the window at the missing man's flowerpots all in a row on the balcony. God would have to water them, I supposed. What in the hell was I doing getting myself involved in this? Maybe Polly could help me get the guy's papers together, but whatever else I thought I was looking for I wasn't going to find. It was a little like visiting your mother's grave and knowing that your mother isn't there.

What could Sergeant Cooperman find in this place, I wondered? And why does Polly Price want me here instead of New York's finest? And where is Derrick Price's car? And is Polly holding back on me or is she merely the traumatized wife bravely holding up as well as can be expected? Lots of little questions. But unlike the rows of ties and flowerpots, I had a feeling some of the answers were going to be messy as hell.

I walked back into the other room just as Polly was collecting some papers for me in a neat little pile on Derrick's desk. She also seemed to have collected herself pretty well.

"Polly," I said, "just as your husband may have gotten into something over his head, so might I have gotten into something over my head with this particular investigation. It looks like the only rational starting point is whatever you've been able to assemble on the desk there, and frankly, computer checks and paper chases aren't really my long suits. The consultant I rely on for that kind of thing is out of the country and I don't know when he's getting back. I want to find your husband. You want to find your husband. But what if your husband doesn't want to be found?"

Polly Price found a cigarette. I lit it for her. I liked to make myself useful.

Then she stacked the papers again neatly and put them in a large yellow envelope and handed it to me. I accepted the envelope reluctantly.

"Do you believe in God?" she said.

"I can't answer that until I talk to my lawyer," I said. "And right now he's missing."

"Don't ask me how I know this," she said. "But you're the one who's going to find Derrick."

Chapter Ten

I took the envelope and the keys to Price's car, walked over to the parking garage down the street, and located the small concrete space where the missing lawyer had probably paid enough a month to rent a nice house almost anywhere else in the country. The car was there. So was I. So I routinely checked the vehicle inside and out for recent dents, bloodstains, anything at all that might help me learn what had happened to Derrick Price. There was nothing. Finally, I took down the license number, returned the keys to one of the nineteen doormen, hailed a passing hack, and headed for Vandam Street.

I had misgivings about staying on the case, but then, I had misgivings about a lot of things in life. One of them was, as my friend Dylan had once observed, how football coaches always used the word "football" in every sentence when they're being interviewed after the game. The season was all but over now, of course, except for the Super Bowl. I was keenly aware that watching pro football was an extremely accurate index of the emptiness of one's life. Nonetheless, I missed absentmindedly watching the players tump over on the field.

Why did Polly Price seem not to want the police to investigate the disappearance of her husband? If they did, would Cooperman's minions have any better chance of finding him than I would? I doubted it. The NYPD, I reflected, probably didn't believe in God either. I might as well lead the charge, I figured. Unless you're the lead dog, the scenery never really changes.

I'd go back to the loft and attempt to sift through Derrick Price's papers. I didn't hold out much hope for really finding anything. I was fairly ill equipped to be some kind of technological, research-oriented, investigative bean counter. And yet it was all that was left. The situation only reinforced my theory that all of us are drawn to occupations that we're horribly ill suited for. It was certainly true of my cabdriver, who ran seven red lights, thought of the sidewalk as his passing lane, and almost collected ten points for hitting an albino Negro who'd made the mistake of trying to legally cross Seventh Avenue.

As the chill of twilight rain stabbed Manhattan, I faced the prospect of a long, lonely evening at the loft. It was a dead time after the holidays, the time when depressed dentists and other Americans often choose to croak themselves, and I was beginning to realize why. Everything I had in my life was on the table. The yellow envelope, yet to be opened. The bottle of Jameson, either half full or half empty, depending on whether you were a country-music line dancer or a depressed dentist. A Texas-shaped ashtray containing a half-smoked cigar that was as dead as my dreams. The old bull's horn, which I liked to think had fatally gored an indecisive matador or two in its day before it moved on to its next incarnation and began its job of fatally goring me. And the cat, who probably expressed my attitude best of all by attempting to scratch, with a high degree of style and irritation, a flea she couldn't find.

I sat down at the empty table. There were no guests, so I could pick any chair I liked. Lots of elbow room for Daniel Boone. I poured a stiff shot and downed it and sat there for a while staring out the grimy kitchen window at the grimy New York night. It almost made you feel grimy just to look at it. Grimy and rainy.

"Better to feel grimy and rainy than nothing at all," I said to the cat.

The cat said nothing but began almost ritually licking herself in an area that was not particularly germane to my current investigation. Or maybe it was. Out of respect for the cat, however, I will reveal the precise locus of her attentions only to those on a need-to-know basis.

I fired up the dead cigar, poured another shot, and sat at the little table staring at the yellow envelope and thinking about my life. My support system had atrophied almost entirely, it seemed. The people who had comforted, helped, and sustained me over the years, both professionally and personally, now all appeared to be far away, busy, or dead. Some of them, very possibly all three. What Doc Phelps, a dear, dead friend of our family, had once remarked about his lonely last years in New Mexico now came to mind. He'd said that he was a very lucky man because he'd loved many people in his life and he still did. I was a lucky man, too, I reflected. But what a strange way to be lucky. But then again, if you thought about it, lucky was always a little strange.

I poured the contents of the bull's horn onto my uvula and poured the contents of the yellow envelope onto the table.

"Okay, Derrick," I said, "I'm settin' my ears back and comin' after you, boy!"

The cat did not find anything remarkable about my statement. She was used to witnessing a man in a loft talking to himself and, on this occasion, did not even deem it necessary to register a mew of distaste.

I sorted through the used confetti of Derrick Price's earthly existence for what seemed to me to be about the length of time it'd probably taken him to acquire it. Going through his credit-card receipts and phone bills reminded me vaguely of the kind of enjoyment I derived from doing taxes. For a post-technological Peter Pan like myself, it was a rather hideous labor.

"Hercules the bean counter," I said to the cat.

The cat said nothing, because she wasn't there. She had moved into the living room and was curled up sound asleep in her rocking chair.

"My support system is atrophying even further," I shouted.

But there was no one to hear me. Not the cat. Not Derrick Price. Not even the lesbian dance class, which, possibly in sympathy with my support system, had apparently taken a brief sabbatical. It was all fine with me. When you're a lucky man, very little else matters. I poured another shot into the bull's horn and moved right along on to Derrick's bank statements. Christ, it was fascinating work.

I'd only been perusing the bank statements for about the lifetime of the sea tortoise when something on that little piece of paper seemed to jump up and bite me on the nose. If a guy like me could see it, I figured, it almost had to be a major discrepancy. But there was no way to mistake it. Derrick Price had done something *really* strange. And for him, I suspected, it had definitely not been very lucky.

I was wholly engrossed in double-checking my discovery when the phones rang. With no little degree of irritation I arose from my chosen chair, walked over to the desk, and picked up the blower on the left with a firm, masculine grip.

"Start talkin'," I said.

"All right," said McGovern, in a voice reverberating with tones of both triumph and fear. "He's out there now looking in the window."

"Who? Where?"

"A guy wearing a fedora and an overcoat, standing out in the rain on my fire escape."

"Maybe it's Gene Kelly."

"I *know* who it is. Can you get over here now?"

"Okay, I'm on my way. But who is he?"

"He's the same fucker—"

An electronic beeping came on the line, quickly followed by a strange, extremely loud series of metallic-sounding clangs.

Then the blower went dead in my hand.

Chapter Eleven

It was pushing Cinderella time when I finally flagged a hack out on Hudson Street. McGovern was at least right about one thing. It was raining like a bitch. I didn't really mind. In fact, after the fashion of W. C. Fields, I truly loved the rain. There is a rather poignant little anecdote, hopefully not apocryphal, about the death of Fields. During the time he was dying, it is said that his much younger lover, actress Carlotta Monti, knowing the great man's fondness for rain on the roof, often went outside, unbeknownst to Fields, and sprayed the roof of the house with a garden hose. With my support system atrophying almost entirely, I reflected, by the time I died there wouldn't be anyone around to spray a garden hose on the roof. There probably wouldn't be anyone around to even *hold* my garden hose. On the other hand, there was a somewhat positive note about the situation. If something in your life had to be atrophying, I thought, far better it be your support system than your garden hose.

About four potholes later, my meditation on the tragic life of W. C. Fields, along with the rain, I noticed, had stopped. My mind now was welling up with thoughts full of angry frustration, almost all of them aimed directly at my old pal McGovern. Whatever the nature of his personal problems, he'd picked a hell of an inconvenient time in which to be experiencing them. He's the last guy in the world you'd ever want in your support system, I thought, and he was just about the only one I still had in mine.

To be totally fair to McGovern, he had many rare, human, almost Christ-like qualities. How a guy like that ever wound up in New York was another question. He was not materialistic like Ratso. Of course, no one was materialistic quite like Ratso. Ratso had materialistic staked out. Stood to inherit slightly under 57 million dollars and didn't want to run up the phone bill calling his old friend over the holidays. Never true of McGovern. McGovern was there when you needed him. Unfortunately, McGovern was also there when you didn't need him.

I paid the hack and legged it up Jane Street past the place where the last windmill in the Village used to stand. As I climbed the steps to McGovern's place, I tried to imagine a guy as big as he was crouching in his bedroom and whispering hoarsely on the telephone so as not to alert the mysterious character who was lurking on his fire escape. It was a mildly humorous picture. Even when McGovern crouched he was bigger than anybody else.

I pressed the buzzer for apartment 2B.

The answering buzz came almost immediately. I jerked open the front door and moved quickly through the little foyer, down the narrow hallway, and up the short stairwell to the second floor. McGovern's place was at the far end of the second-floor hallway, and I could see that his door was slightly ajar. No light was coming from inside his apartment.

I pushed the door open cautiously and waited for my eyes to adjust to the dim light. After a moment or two, Carole Lombard's framed photograph gleamed at me from the brick wall beside McGovern's fireplace.

"MIT . . . MIT," I said softly.

There was no answer.

MIT was a code word McGovern and I often used to remind each other that we were still alive. It was an acronym that stood for "Man in Trouble." The idea had come when McGovern had seen a story on the wire about a guy who'd died in his apartment in Chicago. It'd taken six months before they'd discovered the body and by that time it looked worse than anything the guy who discovered penicillin ever saw through his microscope, whatever the hell his name was. The legendary what's-his-name.

"MIT—MIT—MIT!!" I said again, this time a good bit louder.

"MIT," came the almost grudging reply from a dark corner of the room.

I looked in the direction of the MIT and saw McGovern's large, familiar form slumped motionlessly in his ancient easy chair. In his hand there appeared to be a tall glass of something that my cowboy intuition told me was very likely a rather strong Vodka McGovern.

"Growing hallucinogenic mushrooms, are we?" I said, as I felt around for the light switch. It certainly would've explained McGovern's recent behavior.

"Turn on the lights," said McGovern bitterly. "The party's over."

"Good line for a country song," I said. "I'll see what I can do with it."

"That fucker was there, I tell you, and now he's gone."

"I'm not sure if *that* lyric is quite as commercial."

I found the lights and glanced around McGovern's cluttered living room. It looked like it'd been hit by the Sunset Limited, but as far as I could tell everything was in its usual place, which, of course, was all over the place. McGovern could be criticized for many things but it was refreshing, for some reason, to find a man who was beyond any shadow of the doubt *not* an anal retentive.

"Fucker was right there on the fire escape," said McGovern, like a small, petulant child, used to having the grown-up world not believe his stories.

He pointed stubbornly to the landing of the fire escape, which was plainly visible through the nearby window. It was also plainly visible that no one was standing on the fire escape. Apparently, McGovern had already had more than a few Vodka McGoverns this evening. I was not, of course, in a really good position to be giving him a temperance lecture.

"Let's have a look out there," I said.

"Be my guest."

"I've been your guest, McGovern, on several rather memorable occasions, if you recall."

McGovern laughed for a moment, but I could tell his heart was really not in it. It was a quiet, almost sad laugh, a rare thing indeed for the hard-living, fun-loving Irishman. Possibly, it emanated from the tall, proud Native American side of his family tree.

I walked past McGovern and over to the window that opened onto the fire-escape landing. I started to open it and found that it was locked. Not an unusual thing in New York.

"You normally keep this window locked when you're at home?"

"Only when there's a guy standing on the fire escape."

"Could this guy see you?"

"I don't think so. I was kind of peeking at him through the blinds in the bedroom. He seemed to be looking here into the living room like he was casing out the place."

"You told me on the phone you knew who this

guy is. Who is he?"

"You know that old Indian guy we saw in Myers of Keswick?"

"The one with the receding turban?"

"Abso*loot*ely. I saw him following me yesterday morning without the turban. Then he shows up at Myers of Keswick that evening. Tonight I catch him looking in my window wearing a fedora."

"Curiouser and curiouser."

I unlocked the window and raised it up as far as it would go. I stepped out on the fire-escape landing and looked down at the little alley that ran behind McGovern's building. Not a soul down there. McGovern, like some kind of urban turtle, briefly poked his large head out the window. As I turned toward him I saw what looked like a man's wallet lying on the landing next to the wall. I picked it up and started to check its contents.

"What've you got?" said McGovern from back inside the apartment.

"Michael R. McGovern," I said, reading the driver's license by the lights of the city. I held the wallet up for him to see.

"Hey, that's great!" he said. "I've been looking for that wallet for almost a week!"

"It's dry, you'll note," I said, as I climbed back into the apartment. "When did you first see this guy and when did he leave?"

"When I first saw him it was already raining."

"That'd make it about a half an hour ago."

"Just after it stopped, I looked out again and he was gone. So he must've dropped the wallet right after the rain stopped as he was leaving."

"Yes, Watson, but don't you find it quite singular that he was able to steal the wallet in the first place, considering that the window was locked?"

"He might've taken it earlier in the week."

"And now, like a good little New Yorker, he's bringing it back? I have my doubts about that theory, Watson."

"At least he didn't take any money," said McGovern as he looked through his newly reclaimed property.

"McGovern," I said, as I carefully lit a cigar with the new phlegm-colored Bic that had been in the family for about forty-eight hours, "you and I are men of the world."

"We are?"

"Ah, yes. We live. We love. We will, on occasion, take a drink."

McGovern, I noticed, was already freshening up his Vodka McGovern as I spoke. I continued in what I hoped he would perceive as a rather stern voice. "McGovern, were you at any time tonight out on that fire escape?"

McGovern continued to stir his drink without looking at me, but I could feel him gearing up to drive off in a 1937 Snit. These snits didn't last long, but for their duration there was no use talking to him. If he responded at all, he was usually quite childish, and that was a nice word for it. I puffed on my cigar a bit in the heavy silence, then moved toward the door.

"Say, McGovern," I said, "who was the guy who discovered penicillin?"

"Fleming," he said, rather sulkily. "Alexander Fleming." It was amazing, I thought, that his mind could remember something like that and yet not be able to keep track of his own wallet.

McGovern drank a healthy slug from his tall glass, then turned his back on me to make eye contact with Carole Lombard. He was obviously still smarting from my implication that he might have dropped his own wallet on the fire escape.

"Why do you want to know about Fleming?" he said.

"No reason."

He stared at Carole Lombard for a long while, and since I had nothing else to do, I stared at her, too. She smiled sensuously back at both of us. In fact, she smiled sensuously back at the whole damn world. She knew she met all the criteria. She was funny, beautiful, intelligent, and dead. If you had to fall in love, I thought, she was about the best you could ever hope for.

McGovern had now turned around and appeared to be getting ready to address me. First he took a generous swallow or two of his drink. Then he fixed me with what he felt was his version of a stern gaze.

"Can you take a little constructive criticism?" he said.

"Sure," I said. "Let's hear it."

"Fuck yourself," he said.

Then he laughed. This time it was the real thing.

Chapter Twelve

The first thing in the morning I looked at the clock and realized it was noon. I'd slept relatively well for a change, not experiencing any wet dreams about McGovern's dry wallet, but I had to admit it was still on my mind. The fact of the business, I thought, as I went into the dumper and attended to my various morning ablutions, was that I had to prioritize my work schedule or nothing at all would get done. The whole situation with

McGovern, I had come to realize, was merely a sideshow, but, like any good sideshow, it had stolen my attention away from the really important matters at hand: finding my battery-operated nose-hair clippers and finding Derrick Price.

Nose hairs are something you don't think about much until you reach middle age, and then they seem to take over your life. Looking at things from the other nostril, Derrick Price was going to be one tough little booger to find. I finally had a lead and I planned to start checking it out as soon as I'd fed the cat, jump-started the espresso machine, and set fire to my first cigar of the day. But I wasn't all that optimistic about it. Of course, I wasn't all that optimistic about anything.

I'd spent enough time playing cops and robbers with Sergeant Cooperman and Sergeant Fox and Rambam and my private-investigator friend in L.A., Kent Perkins. From them I'd learned the conventional, and occasionally unconventional, wisdom about missing person cases. If you didn't find the person within the first week or so, you'd better be prepared to spend your lifetime looking for him. Somehow I didn't think Polly Price's retainer, or her patience, or even her newfound religiosity would last that long. As for my own beliefs, I did not think that God wanted me to spend my life searching for some mysteriously misplaced lawyer. I listened to the still, small voice within and suddenly, very possibly for the first time in my life, I heard clearly the Lord's commandment to me. I understood what He wanted me to do. God wanted me to find my battery-operated nose-hair clippers.

"God," I said, as I went back into the dumper, cigar in hand, to take a large Nixon, "a man's life may be at stake and I think I've finally got a hot lead to run down that may help me find him. Why in the hell would you want me running around looking for nose-hair clippers?" It sounded like a fairly reasonable question for a mortal to ask.

"Cleanliness is next to godliness," said the still, small voice. The Lord was obviously no respecter of persons, whether missing or trying to take a Nixon.

"Look," I said, "I'm kind of busy right now. One thing at a time. Let me finish laying some cable here and then I'll jump in the rain room for you. Be cleaner than the whole damn continent of Europe."

Actually, I had no intention at all of taking a shower. For one thing, the cat's litter box was always kept in the rain room, and if I wanted to take a shower I'd have to move it out. This could prove mildly unpleasant, seeing as I hadn't changed the litter in so long that some of the turds had fossilized and now were beginning to resemble rare pre-Columbian artifacts. This, of itself, was not entirely bad. If things ever really got rough, there always existed the possibility of putting them on the market. I felt pretty sure some New York art dealer would snap them right up. This wasn't the time, however. There was all kinds of crap on the market right now and, whatever happened, I didn't want to sell short.

"Frank Sinatra washes his hands five times a day," said the still, small voice, ever eager to make its point. Like a great number of biblical characters, I continued to smoke a cigar and take a Nixon and pretended not to hear the voice. This effort at normal daily behavior on my part wasn't about to stop God, however. If anything, it only seemed to encourage Him.

"Stephanie DuPont takes three showers a day," saith the voice, becoming positively garrulous now.

"Why you ol' devil," I said good-naturedly, "you've been watching, haven't you?"

There are times when you feel close to God and times when you don't and there are times when the two of you need to get away from each other for a while. I finished my paperwork in the dumper, washed my hands one time, grabbed a cup of steaming espresso, and headed for the kitchen table to tackle my other paperwork. Maybe I was being a bit curt, but I didn't have time to sit around heaven all day watching every nose-hair clipper, sparrow, and Hutu machete. I felt fairly sure that God, once He'd had a chance to think about it, would understand that I needed to get busy being my brother's keeper. You never knew, I figured. One of these days you might just find that your brother's name is Derrick Price.

Chapter Thirteen

Like Columbus, it took me quite a while to reach the Bank of America. And that was only the beginning of the journey. I was working with a canceled check that Price had written on his own local bank the week before he'd disappeared. It was made out to the Inter-America Trading and Finance Corporation to the tune of one hundred and fifty thousand dollars. The amount and the timing of the check made it stand out from the rest of Price's transactions like a Jew with an ant farm.

The basic method I planned to adopt in order

to establish a paper trail was what Rambam often spoke of as his "hard-boiled computer" approach. I didn't have a computer and Rambam was still in Tel Aviv, London, or Sri Lanka, but otherwise, I figured, the damn thing ought to work. So, from the information on the back of the check I called the local Bank of America office and asked for the location of their branch #282. They spit it back to me with all due haste. It was in Fairfax, Virginia. I was on a roll.

Now I picked up the blower and called information in Fairfax, Virginia, for the local Bank of America branch, called the bank, and held on while I was shunted between underlings until I reached a customer service corporate accounts type of individual.

"My name is Derrick Price," I said. "I'm calling from New York."

"Gladys Hemoglobin," she said. "How can I help you?"

"I'm with Schmeckel & Schmeckel and I need to make a second payment to one of your corporate customers, Inter-America Trading and Finance. What I need is their mailing address. My secretary managed to leave the file in Hong Kong."

"One moment, please, Mr. Price."

I winked at the cat and waited. This was so easy you could do it at home.

A short while later she came back on the line and gave me an address in Silver Spring, Maryland. I thanked her, hung up the blower, lit a fresh cigar, and restocked myself in the espresso department. Then I called information in Silver Spring for the Inter-America Trading and Finance Corporation.

There was no listing.

51

Now I had a mailing address for the corporation but no listing for their phone number. I could have someone in the area check out the address for me or, as Rambam would say, I could "develop a new address." The latter sounded like the way to go. I didn't know what kind of dark venture Derrick Price was up to or caught up in—blackmail, extortion, embezzlement. Any one of them might be enough to make your average American hop the next flight on Qantas, the Rainman's favorite airline, with a one-way ticket to Malabimbi. Provided, of course, that somebody hadn't already punched your ticket.

Whether you considered the "hard-boiled computer" method of investigative work fascinating or tedious, or a little of both, it had one rather large advantage over the standard physical gumshoe approach. It was better for your health, education, and welfare to be smoking a cigar and sipping an espresso in your loft than it was to be lurking in a freezing, rain-wept alleyway by some shipyard watching a warehouse door out of which at any moment might emerge a thousand clowns, all of them named John Wayne Gacy.

So it was an easy decision, if it was at all possible, to keep the long, long paper trail winding into the land of my dreams. Stymied temporarily by the lack of a phone number for the Silver Spring address, I set about developing a new address for the Inter-America Trading and Finance Corporation. I called the Maryland Secretary of State's Office, Division of Corporations. I had now assumed the identity of your basic everyday process server, an individual that, according to Rambam again, is "very low on the food chain and will arouse no suspicion." Indeed, the petty functionaries I spoke to at the Secretary of State's office did appear to regard me as little more than a rather commonplace nuisance. A real process server probably gets used to this shabby treatment. For me, however, it was a hell of a step down from my secretary leaving the files in Hong Kong.

"An out-of-state service address," remarked one bureaucrat, after I'd been passed around for ten minutes like an Olympic baton. "Very unusual."

"I've never seen anything like it," I said—the most truthful words I'd uttered all day.

"I don't even know if it's legal," said the bureaucrat noncommittally, a natural timbre of ennui beginning to return to his voice.

"That's what keeps me in business," I said, trying for a little enthusiasm to further feed his lack of interest. It worked.

When I hung up the blower I had the name and phone number of a Washington, D.C., law firm that ostensibly served as the service address for the corporation to which Derrick Price had recently paid out one hundred and fifty thousand dollars. I kind of preferred blackmail, but by this time, fraud, extortion, or embezzlement all would've been fine. Anything to lead me to the king.

"We're closing in on this bird," I said to the cat, using a metaphor I knew she could relate to. The cat blinked several times and seemed to be taking a renewed interest in the proceedings, which I hoped were finally leading somewhere, because by this time they'd become extremely tedioso.

I called the law firm in Washington as a representative of the Acme Process Service with a summons and complaint on the Inter-American Trade and Finance Corporation. I was transferred to somebody's administrative secretary, who seemed to have at least twenty seconds for me.

"Are you still the valid service address for Inter-America?" I said.

"No," she said. "There's a new valid service address. Just a moment."

I waited. I put my boots up on the desk, puffed the cigar, and took a little break like any tired cowboy along the old paper trail.

"Any legal papers," she said, coming back on the line, "should be served on Roscoe West." Then she gave me another address in Washington.

I called information and got the phone number. Then I called the number. It rang and rang and rang.

Repeatedly, for the rest of the day, I called the number in Washington with no results. Nobody was home and I was past developing a new address because probably nobody would be home there either. There's very little flesh and blood along a paper trail. You might meet a paper doll. She might live beside a cardboard sea. And yet something told me instinctively that I was getting fairly close to my target. I had an address. I had a working phone number. Once I came down from feeling like I'd spent most of my adult life manning the phone banks at the Jerry Lewis Facial Tic Telethon, I might well be able to move forward actively with the investigation.

Later that evening I made one final phone call to Polly Price. She seemed much more in control of herself than she had the day before.

"Any progress?" she wanted to know.

I filled her in as much as I thought was appropriate, which was not too much, and I gave her a slightly more positive spin on the thing than I, at the moment, felt.

"A lead's a lead," I said, "and it's the best we've got. So I'm haulin' buns for Washington in the morning."

"That's funny," she said.

"Haulin' buns?"

"No," she said tonelessly.

"What is it, Polly?"

"Derrick used to love Washington, but in the past year he's been avoiding it like the plague. These days we always seem to be getting together in New York."

"That's interesting," I said.

"Whatever you find out, Kinky—whatever trouble he may be in—I want to know. Promise you'll tell me. Whatever it is."

"I promise. When I know something, you'll know."

To be totally truthful, I thought I knew something already. What I knew was that Polly knew something. Why else would a distraught woman who'd mislaid her husband not want the police involved? Maybe she had dark suspicions of her own. Maybe she knew what kind of trouble he was in. Maybe she wanted to protect his reputation from his partners at the firm.

But for whatever the reason, not unlike many a bird in a gilded cage, Polly wasn't talking. If she had, it might've saved a handful of Americans from a worldful of grief.

Chapter Fourteen

The shuttle from La Guardia flew low over the Potomac in preparation for landing in Washington, the city where William Henry Harrison steadfastly refused to wear his overcoat for his inaugural parade. He died about two weeks later of pneumonia. I wasn't about to make the same mistake. I wore a heavy blue peacoat that looked like it'd been handed down to me by Oliver Twist along with a bright red Sydney Swans Australian football scarf and a black cowboy hat. I might not blend in too well at some of the more upscale restaurants, but it's always better to look like a squirrel, I figured, than it is to freeze your nuts off.

Because of Washington Ratso's time-consuming job as news cameraman for Channel 9 and my own time-consuming job of being an unemployed youth, I hadn't actually spoken to him since the moment Polly Price had first held my puppet head. I had left a few messages on his machine, he'd left a few messages on my machine, and that had been about the extent of both of our contributions recently to peace in the Middle East. Ratso was a Lebanese Druse, a tribe of people, not unlike the Jews, who only seemed to fit in where they didn't belong.

I'd first met Jimmie "Ratso" Silman in 1978 when I was playing a gig at the Cellar Door in Georgetown. He was then performing with the great rockabilly legend Tex Rabinowitz and the Bad Boys. At the time, I was working with only a guitar player, so Ratso had consented, sight unheard, to sit in on bass. After the first set, I had apparently decided to jet the guitar player for some reason, so I told Ratso I didn't need a bass player. He moved over to guitar for the second set. After the second set I decided I didn't need another guitar player. Not too long after that, I realized I didn't even really need myself.

Yet Ratso and I had remained close friends. We'd performed together sporadically over the years, musically speaking, at Willie Nelson picnics, the Lone Star Cafe, the famous Mo & Joe's Steakhouse, and the occasional whorehouse or bar mitzvah. We never made the White House, but then again, neither did Adlai Stevenson.

Now, as I stepped out of the airport onto the cold chill of the sidewalk, I lit a cigar and scanned a stormy sea of agitated faces. It looked like the entire United Nations was waiting in line for the same taxicab, but I did not see Ratso among them. So I stood on the curb and smoked the cigar and nodded as two friendly-looking Sikhs walked by. Those are always the best kind.

"Kinkster!" came a loud voice from somewhere amongst my fellow-passengers to the grave. "Over here!"

Once I saw him he was hard to miss. Ratso was wearing a big black cowboy hat like my own and a thick, general-issue Iraqi-type mustache. Under the mustache was one of the biggest smiles this side of Watergate. He was driving a mobile media arsenal with antennae and satellite dishes all over it and Channel 9 News scrawled across the side in bright red letters.

"Your limo's here, sir," he said, as I climbed into the front seat alongside him. "And welcome to your nation's capital."

"And all this time I thought it was Austin," I said.

"That was before Ann Richards lost."

Ratso put the van into gear and before I knew it, he was weaving the bold, yet intricate embroidery required to get out of any modern airport alive.

"Now if you'll just tell me where the hell we're going," said Ratso, "and possibly why."

I tore the address out of my little private investigator's notebook and handed it to Ratso.

"Not my usual beat," said Ratso, glancing at the address. "It's in a nice neighborhood."

"Right. So what did Polly Price tell you?"

"Not a hell of a lot."

"Funny. That's the same thing she told me."

"Nice nay-nays, though."

"Ah, your roaming Bedouin eye caught that, did it?"

"Roger. And I'd like to get the nose of my camel into her tent."

"Cheer up. She thinks you're a fine, clean-cut, upstanding gentleman and you may get your chance as soon as I don't find her husband."

"You'll find him, Kinkster. I've got faith in you."

"Faith in me? I thought you were supposed to have faith in Allah."

"Allah," said Ratso dismissively. "I gave up on Allah when the Redskins lost to Tampa Bay."

As we headed toward the city, both of us wearing black cowboy hats and smoking big cigars, we looked, I thought, very much like the biblical brothers we no doubt were if anybody ever bothered to climb our family trees high enough to find the olive branch. Just as the traffic began getting more congested, Ratso's three police and fire scanners started speaking in tongues.

"*Motor Twenty-three*," said one scanner.

"What's that?" I said.

"That's nothing," said Ratso. "It takes a while to develop scanner ears."

"*Motor Twenty-three.*"

"*Respond to gunshots seven hundred block of Eighth*

Street, N.E."

"*Response?*"

"*Code one.*"

"What's code one?" I said.

"Lights and siren," said Ratso.

"What's code two?"

"Lights only."

"What's code three?"

"No anchovies," said Ratso, as the van hurtled across the Fourteenth Street Bridge.

"What's that?" I said, pointing over to the left.

"Jefferson Memorial. Sorry there's no cherry blossoms this time of year. Japan's gift of peace and friendship to the American people."

"I thought it was karaoke."

As the neighborhoods changed kaleidoscopically from Beverly Hills to Calcutta and back again in a heartbeat, Ratso and I drove through the mean streets of our nation's capital, smoking cigars, discussing the possible whereabouts of Derrick Price, and half-listening to the almost nonstop chatter of the scanners.

"*Gunshot wound in the lower back—*"

"That means his ass," said Ratso.

"*What hospital is the victim going to?*" asked a dispatcher.

"*The victim is unconscious—*"

"That means he's dead," said Ratso. "We're getting close to our address. What's the name of the guy again?"

"Roscoe West. But I don't think he'll be there, whoever the hell he is. It'll probably be the Latvian embassy or something. More than likely, ol' podner, this is the end of our little paper trail."

"Don't forget to recycle."

As we closed in on our destination, Ratso slowed

the van and we gazed around to see block after block of wide, peaceful streets, large expanses of lawns, and graceful World War II era houses, many of them old mansions.

"Roscoe West appears to be farting through silk," said Ratso, as he slowed down even further and began looking for the address.

"Not what I expected," I said.

Suddenly, in stark contrast to our genteel and, quite possibly gentile, surroundings, all three scanners exploded in terse commands, grunts, shouts, and raucous white noise. It sounded a bit as if the trio of communication devices had somehow achieved the effect of a ménage à trois reaching simultaneous sexual climax.

"What the hell is going on?"

"That's the code for officer in trouble," said Ratso. "All hell breaks loose, people running, total pandemonium, cars driving on sidewalks. We call that a ten thirty-three."

"I've heard of that," I said, "but we have another name for it."

"What do you call it?" said Ratso, pulling up in front of the address.

"We call it New York," I said.

Chapter Fifteen

A freezing rain had started to fall as Ratso and I, like two friendly cowboy Jehovah's Witnesses, eased up the walkway to the old mansion. The dark, stormy weather added a bleak countenance to the place which had already been redlining in the Lon Chaney department to begin with. Ratso's TV news van was parked down the street, and

60

with another tedious Christmas season already thankfully in the side pocket, there still did not seem to be a creature stirring in the immediate vicinity. But appearances, like people, could be deceiving. So, like good little Jehovah's Witnesses, we masked our zealous persistence with an infuriatingly patient demeanor.

We observed the three brass plates beside the door. One of them read: Roscoe West and Associates.

"Looks like the place," said Ratso.

"It also looks like all the little lobbyists and lawyers are still on their holiday skiing trip to Upper Baboon's Asshole, Colorado."

"How come you and I never go to those places, Kinkster?"

"Because some of us work for a living," I said.

"You've never had a job in your life."

"I said *some* of us work for a living."

During the course of this little repartee we'd walked over to several of the front windows and observed that, indeed, the old place did seem rather void of human habitation. So, having rung the bell at Roscoe West and Associates with no apparent response, we turned the old knob, gave the big door a push, found to our surprise that it was unlocked, and walked inside.

The wings to our left and our right were dark and silent, but from the Roscoe West suite, which apparently was upstairs, there seemed to come faint scurrying sounds. It could've been rats, people, or my imagination, any of which had the potential to be rather unpleasant. Then the faint noises ceased and it was silent again all through the house.

"Up the stairs, Goldilocks?" asked Ratso.

"Lead the caravan on, my brave Arabian brother."

"Oh no, my wise Hebraic elder. This is your gig."

It certainly wasn't breaking and entering, since the front door had been unlocked, but as we climbed the darkened stairs, I felt an increasing sense of not belonging there pervade what little was left of my conscience. The mere possession of a conscience, I reflected, can be a somewhat severe handicap, both in the field of crime detection and, of course, in Washington.

At the top of the stairs we walked through an open door into a large suite of offices. No one seemed to be around, but the lights were on. I gave a few halfhearted shouts of greeting and we waited. Nothing. Empty bureaucratic canyons.

"Maybe somebody just accidentally left the lights on," said Ratso.

"And the door unlocked?"

I walked into Roscoe West's office and did a bit of exploring as Ratso wandered farther along the adjoining rooms. A quick search through West's filing cabinet revealed no Derrick Price file. That would've been too easy, I thought. But as I was leaving the office I heard a slight humming sound. It seemed to be emanating from a nearby desk. It was a typewriter left in the "on" position. In the carriage was what appeared to be a half-written business letter of some sort. I was just beginning to check out the letter when I heard a shout from down the hall.

"Kinkster!" said Ratso. "You better come over here."

As I walked down the long hallway toward Ratso, I noticed something out of place. A phone had been left off the hook. I picked up the wayward blower and tried to listen over Ratso's persistent shouting. All I could hear were unintelligible background conversations that sounded vaguely like what I'd been hearing in Ratso's news van.

"Where in the hell did everybody go?" I said, as I entered the doorway of the small storage room in which Ratso was standing. "Did someone declare World War III and decide not to tell us about it?"

Ratso didn't answer. He was standing behind a small table staring down at what appeared to be a medium-sized half-open suitcase.

"We're certainly dealing with a rather forgetful crew," I said. "They left the lights on. They left a typewriter running. They left a phone off the hook—"

"That's not all they left," said Ratso.

I walked around the table and gazed transfixedly down at a whole suitcase full of clear bags of white powder. Whiter than snowflakes. Shinier than fish scales. The ashes of my misbegotten youth.

"If that's cocaine," said Ratso, "there's enough there to send your penis to Venus."

"Probably several times," I said. "As Mrs. Henry Cabot Lodge once remarked: 'If you took everybody who fell asleep in church and put them end-to-end in a line on the floor, they'd be much more comfortable.'"

"Until you snorted the line," said Ratso.

I stood over the white stuff like I was looking over my open grave. I didn't know whether to curse or pray as my mind went back a million years to a sometimes celestial sometimes nightmarish world that Nancy Reagan, for better or worse, would never know. Moments of magic, decades of destruction, fragile, tender, star-crossed, deathbound, heroic, beautiful, hopeless, immortal. From the Wichita Lineman to *Twenty Thousand Leagues Under the Sea* and back again, before the time of my first Black Mary, which is a fairly degenerate drink consisting of one part vodka, one part Bloody Mary mix, and one part Worcestershire sauce. Dancing with angels, struggling with demons, understanding finally the wisdom of the Roger Miller song my friend Captain Midnite once sent me: "Don't Write Letters to My Dog." If this shit was Peruvian marching powder, it could make the whole city of Los Angeles so high that it'd start to get lonely. If this shit was heroin, there was enough here to create a whole new galaxy of dead rock 'n' roll stars. Whatever this shit was, its street value was just about whatever you thought your life was worth. If this supply ran out before you did, the only possible greater high would be for you to chop up and snort Nancy Reagan.

Without even touching the stuff in the suitcase I was now seeing vague flashes of red and blue light on the far wall of the storage room.

"We've been set up!" shouted Ratso, running to the nearest window, then scampering back at twice the pace. "There's a sea of squad cars down there with their lights flashing. How in the hell did they slip up on us like this?"

"Obviously code two," I said.

Chapter Sixteen

From a frozen fire escape in back, through the open window, we could hear the sounds of the cops storming the stairs. The whole experience still seemed like something from a movie. The kind you wanted to get up and walk out of. In this case, run. Of course we'd been set up. How and by whom I'd try to figure out later. If there was a later.

Just as most of us operate our brains on about one cylinder much of the time, our true athletic prowess is a component of our being that is also often unknown to us. Ratso and I scooted down that fire escape faster than God makes fat ladies at the supermarket. We ran across the sprawling back lawns of the mansion, across the little delivery drive, and through a thick hedgerow of bushes that had, almost miraculously, retained their green foliage. Maybe God had had something to do with that, too, foreseeing Ratso's and my need for concealment as we wandered rather quickly through the spiritual desert of Washington. If God had indeed been busy creating fat ladies in the supermarket and leaves on this hedgerow, it could account for why the rest of the world seemed to be going inexorably to hell. Yet we needed a God, I thought, in passing yet another yard and another hedgerow. Without Him there would be no one to curse. And I certainly wasn't about to deny His existence at this time. No man is an atheist when he's running for his life.

The body runs fast, but the mind runs faster. Why leave the phone off the hook, I wondered? Had somebody set us up by placing a call to the cops or by dialing 911? If so, leaving the blower off the hook would be an effective way to make sure the lead was followed up. Maybe we had been set up. Maybe I was closer than I thought to finding Derrick Price. But why would it be so important for someone to try to hinder my investigation in this matter? And who could possibly afford to leave that ungodly amount of Irving Berlin's White Christmas lying around in a suitcase merely to attempt to implicate me?

It was quite ridiculous. Of course, it was also ridiculous to be running blithely through the grounds of neighboring estates in an effort to elude the division of cops who were now streaming onto the fire escape. I heard them shouting but I didn't stop. I was on autopilot and I suddenly felt a giddy flash of childhood clotheslines and garbage cans and forts made from discarded Christmas trees. Ratso had swiftly metamorphosed into my long-ago friend Steve Worchel, and the two of us were speeding through the backyards of the 1950s and of summertime in Austin, Texas. We'd just thrown some rocks at a yellowjacket's nest and were running for our lives much in the manner that one part of my mind still knew Ratso and I were running for our lives. No matter who you are, running for your life can be dangerous, stressful, tiresome work, I reflected very briefly, but it sure beats jogging.

"Are you okay?" Steve Worchel was asking me.

But I wasn't. My right arm was hurting terribly. Six years into the charade of life and nothing had hurt this bad.

"You got bit!" Steve shouted in total six-year-old panic.

"What?" I said, in total six-year-old confusion.

Then the veil of childhood was suddenly lifted and Steve Worchel became Jimmie "Ratso" Silman and more than forty years had gone over the goddamn dam and I was leaning against a rock wall and men were shouting somewhere on the other side.

"You got hit!" said Ratso. "But I think we can make it to the truck from here. Rest a moment and then we'll make a break for it."

Blood was now beginning to stain my Oliver Twist coat, but I felt strangely at peace.

"How do you feel?" asked Ratso, with what seemed like six thousand years of biblical brotherhood in his brown eyes.

"As the Spider Woman whispered to Raul Julia," I said, "'This dream is short. But this dream is happy.'"

Chapter Seventeen

What had stung me this time was a hell of a lot worse than what had stung me forty years ago. This time it was a cop's bullet. Or maybe you could call it a modern, grown-up, technological yellowjacket. But somehow Ratso and I made it up a narrow driveway and into the news truck. Ratso tied a strip of cloth tightly and quickly around my arm, which, fortunately for me, the bullet had gone right through. I was taking a little power nap in the backseat when I heard Ratso's voice drifting through the hole in the ozone layer around my brain.

"Goddamnit, they've surrounded the whole neighborhood. They've set up some kind of a perimeter."

"How do you know?"

"They're talking about it on the scanner. The only reason we got to the truck was that some homeless guy was stumbling around in the vicinity and they went after him by mistake."

"Possibly Lazarus," I said, wincing with a sudden jolt of pain as I tried to sit up.

"Stay down in the backseat," said Ratso. "They know they've got the wrong guy now. But I've got an idea and if it works we'll be out of here quick."

"And if it doesn't?"

"I think it'll work. It's always worked in the past."

"What if I bleed to death while we're finding out?"

"Then we may need Allah's services after all, but I don't think it's going to happen. I've seen a lot of wounds before on this job. Yours looks fairly clean and I know a nice little Lebanese doctor."

"I hope he has some magic rocket beans," I said, holding my arm. "It feels like I've just been crucified by Mr. Magoo."

"Just cover yourself with that blanket and stay out of sight. The Rat Man's in charge."

This declaration of bravado did not particularly instill great confidence in me, but I was not in a really good position to argue. In fact, from my recumbent locus in the backseat under the blanket, I couldn't see what Ratso was doing or even begin to guess what he had in mind. Probably that was just as well.

"Hold on to your yarmulke!" shouted Ratso, as the vehicle careened over the curb, sending hot arrows of pain up my right arm.

I grasped the seat as best I could and prayed to whatever gods resided in the sullen skies above Washington, D.C. From my somewhat limited vantage point it appeared as if Ratso was attempting to perform a U-turn and aim the van back in the direction of the old mansion we'd just narrowly escaped from and which now, no doubt, would be swarming with angry cops, one of whose belt was now one bullet lighter.

"Don't go anywhere!" shouted Ratso.

"That's what they told Emily Dickinson."

Ratso accelerated, then skidded to a sudden stop, and before I could grit my teeth, he was out the door and running toward the house with the television camera on his shoulder. It was pure genius. I couldn't see anything, but I could hear the cops very aggressively giving him the bum's rush out of there. In no time at all, Ratso was back behind the wheel feigning great disappointment as the cops unceremoniously escorted us down the street and out of the neighborhood. There were, after all, I reflected, some advantages to being with the media.

"Not only were we lucky to get *out*," said Ratso, some hours later as we relaxed at his apartment, "we were also quite lucky that Dr. Fouad was *in*."

"It certainly was preferable to loitering around some hospital emergency room with cops checking us out and then being slowly done to death by skinny Jewish doctors and fat black nurses like the ones who killed Libby Zion in New York."

"Be careful what you say here in our nation's capital," said Ratso. "Your remarks could be construed as being politically incorrect."

"So could the colored men sign over the door of your dumper."

I looked around the place and realized that not only was I a two-Ratso man, but both Ratsos inhabited extremely eccentric apartments. Of course, Washington Ratso still had a ways to go before catching up with New York Ratso, but that didn't mean he wasn't trying. Maybe if your name was Ratso you just liked to collect weird things and live like a pack rat. On the other hand, if your name was Kinky, what did that indicate that you might like to collect? Always excluding grief, of course. I did not want to ponder too hard on these theories, and, thanks to Dr. Fouad's rocket beans, I didn't have to. My mind, like that of a television talk show host, didn't seem to stay on any one subject for very long.

"How many guitars are in this apartment?" I asked.

"Twelve," said Ratso. "I had to sell two."

"Sorry to hear that. How many snakes do you have?"

"Seven," said Ratso, standing proudly beside a number of nearby glass cages. "They're American king snakes and I've given them all names that have something to do with the King."

"King Herod?"

"No. The American king. Elvis."

"Very nice," I said, watching the large creatures weave their bodies against the other side of the glass.

"This is Elvis," said Ratso, pointing out the largest snake. "This is Priscilla. This one's Lisa Marie. This is Colonel Tom. This is Scotty Moore, Elvis's guitar player. This is D. J. Fontana, Elvis's drummer. I haven't named the seventh one yet."

"Well," I said, "there's time."

"Right now it's time for you to get some rest. Do those painkillers seem to be kicking in yet?"

"They're working kind of slowly," I said, as I lay back on the couch. "Of course, they don't have much of a pension plan."

I watched the snakes for a while. Then I watched the guitars. Then I wondered who could afford to leave behind half a million bucks' worth of marching powder just to try to keep me from finding

Derrick Price. Just before the rocket beans took my head into orbit, I thought I had the answer. But when I woke in the morning, it was gone. A few hours later, so was I.

Chapter Eighteen

For a Lebanese Druse, I reflected on the shuttle flight to New York, Ratso was certainly a fine American. He'd risked his very life for me and had not complained once about all the tedium and trouble I'd dragged him into. He'd been a wonderful Dr. Watson, and, possibly more importantly, he'd been a wonderful friend. Why was this Ratso different from all other Ratsos, I wondered? And what else can you give a guy who already has twelve guitars and seven American king snakes?

I took a few more of Dr. Fouad's rocket beans on the plane and the pain in my arm settled down to a dull throb. I could live with that. I just wasn't sure I would be alive much longer if I kept aggressively investigating the disappearance of Derrick Price. Again and again I came back to the perplexing question of why someone had gone to so much trouble to try to set me up. If I'd been getting that close to finding Price, I wished someone would tell me about it. Maybe, I thought, that was exactly what somebody was trying to do. Whether Price was alive or dead I still didn't know, but I was beginning to plunk for alive.

With my head swirling in confusion and my arm beginning to ache again, I hailed a hack at La Guardia and rode it all the way to Vandam Street. I kept my eye on the blurry big-city scenery and tried not to think too much. I hated to admit it, but it felt good to be back in New York. Now all I had to do was make a report to Polly Price and decide how best to proceed with the investigation, provided she didn't want to take me off the case and replace me with McCloud.

I paid the driver, opened the door of the building, and rode up to the fourth floor in the old freight elevator with the one exposed lightbulb. I slipped my arm out of the little sling that Dr. Fouad had provided and observed it carefully. The arm was still there, all right. It just felt like it belonged on the freight elevator. I put it back in the sling and did a pretty fair one-handed job of opening the door to the loft and carrying my suitcase across the threshold.

"Honey, I'm home," I said.

The cat did not look particularly pleased to see me. Cats rarely do, of course. As young kittens, they were probably never allowed to laugh or cry or to express other intrinsically sensitive feline emotions. This, no doubt, was the main reason why some cats, as well as most people, once they grew up, seemed to turn into assholes. Or, very possibly, they were just born that way.

In stark contrast to the cat, I noticed, the puppet head on the top of the refrigerator was smiling broadly at me from the moment I entered the doorway. This was a bit peculiar, I thought, because, to the best of my knowledge, I'd left the puppet head facing the far wall, looking away from the door of the loft.

I got out a can of Southern Gourmet Dinner for the cat, who now seemed to be warming up a bit to my presence in the loft. Then I looked more closely at the puppet head, which now stood almost in profile to me. I glanced around the loft for a moment, but everything else seemed to be exactly as I'd left it. Only the puppet head had changed its position. Maybe it had gotten bored with the view of the far wall. The wall was covered almost entirely with a huge American flag that had been given to me years ago by Vaughn Meader. Possibly the puppet head's actions could be construed as unpatriotic.

Now I took the puppet head from the top of the refrigerator and stood by the window holding it in my hand like Yorick's skull. Gazing at its friendly countenance more closely, I remembered that the puppet head had been wounded, too, some years earlier, when a stray bullet from a Colombian drug cartel member had struck it during a late night shootout in the loft.

Nonetheless, I'd painstakingly glued it back together and, with the passage of time, the wound was now visible only upon very close inspection. I wasn't sure if it was a healthy thing to empathize with a little black puppet head, but at the moment, the two of us seemed like blood brothers. After all, we had a lot in common. We both had spent a great deal of time alone. We both continued to face the cold world with a brave smile. And for the many good works performed by the puppet head and myself, all either of us had to show for it was that each of us had caught a bullet. Of course, I reflected, his had only been a head wound.

I took a few more of Dr. Fouad's rocket beans and washed them down with some Irish whiskey to possibly give myself a little buzz. Then I went over to the desk and checked out the blower traffic for the past twenty-four hours. There were five messages on the answering machine. One was from Rambam, who was now back in town but was sleeping it off and didn't want to be disturbed for forty-eight hours.

"Reinforcements!" I shouted to the cat.

The cat looked at me as if I were clinically ill.

The next message was from Stephanie DuPont, who was calling from the Concorde as she was coming into Kennedy. There was a lot of static in the background, but it sounded promising.

"The love interest returns!" I shouted to the cat.

The cat absorbed the exciting news and then began licking herself repeatedly in a rather intimate area.

"Anything's possible," I said.

The remaining three calls were from McGovern. All three were MIT calls and each one seemed to become progressively more frantic. Apparently McGovern had been receiving more, and increasingly threatening, phone calls from Leaning Jesus.

I planned to call him back, of course, but first I felt compelled to report in, regardless of the unresolved nature of my findings, to Polly Price. She was, after all, my client of record. My real client. My paying client. McGovern and whatever madness, real or imagined, he was involved in, would have to take a backseat in the family DeSoto.

I dialed Polly's number, and while her phone was ringing, I reached over with my good arm to open the side drawer of the desk. I accomplished this without too much difficulty, but when I looked down into the drawer there was a little surprise waiting for me.

All of Derrick Price's bank statements, records, and papers were missing.

"Hello," said Polly Price.

"I'm glad I got you," I said. "I was afraid I'd misplaced your number."

"What happened in Washington?" she wanted to know. All business now.

"Look, I was wondering if we could get together tonight. You know, socially. Maybe have a few drinks—"

"Listen," she said. "My husband's missing and I don't know if he's in danger or what harm has come to him. I believed in you and put my faith in you to find him. And you want to get together *socially* and have a few drinks? Just what kind of a woman do you think I am?"

"I'll pick you up about eight," I said.

Chapter Nineteen

Maybe I was missing something, I thought. Besides Derrick Price's papers, which had been recently removed from my loft, and the ounce of flesh, which had been recently removed from my right arm. If there was something Polly Price wasn't telling me, it was about a quarter past time to find out. Someone had set Ratso and myself up in Washington. Someone who knew or strongly suspected I was coming to the address of Roscoe West and Associates. That's why the cocaine had been left there. That was why the phone had been left off the hook after someone, no doubt, had called in the tip to 911. By leaving the blower off the hook, they'd insured that the 911 operators, who, according to Rambam, were even lower on the food chain than process servers, would get the message and eventually send someone to the address.

After flipping the thing over in my brainpan for a while, I concluded that was how the setup was set up. Now all I needed to figure out was why. Aside from myself and the cat, only two people knew I was even going to Washington—Ratso and Polly Price. But neither of them could've known the details of my visit. Ratso only learned the address I was going to once I'd gotten in the van at the airport. And Polly had known almost nothing of my plan of action in the nation's capital.

The logical explanation for the setup was that someone I'd talked to along the paper trail had gotten wise and alerted someone else who'd alerted someone else and if Ratso's aggressive on-camera media approach hadn't worked, we'd both probably still be sitting in the calaboose looking for our shoelaces. It is one of the unfortunate aspects of being a private investigator that you must suspect everyone, whether he or she may be one of your oldest friends or even your recently grief-stricken client.

As an amateur detective, you almost have to make it a way of life to suspect everyone around you. This pattern of behavior may not prove to be brick and mortar to your interpersonal relationships, but it is an ancient, trusted, Holmesian method of crime solving that is almost as infallible as a pope on a bloody rope. You probably won't be left with many friends, but at least you'll be left with the truth. The truth, of course, can often be the world's most tedious, stultifyingly dull companion, but such is the lonely, monastic life of the amateur detective.

After meditating on these matters for a while, I finally got off my buttocks and carefully checked out the door and the windows of the loft. I noticed no new marks on the locks and no signs of entry anywhere. A very professional job. And its only purpose appeared to be to steal the papers my client had recently given me. Tonight I would have to find out if Polly had spoken to anyone about Derrick's papers, or even told anyone that she'd hired me to investigate.

"You didn't see anyone?" I said to the cat in a semi-accusatorial manner. "Maybe somebody who came in here late last night, looked around carefully, went through the desk, and removed a big yellow envelope? Then the person went over to the refrigerator and examined the puppet head? Did you see anyone like that?"

The cat did not respond and obviously did not care. She was quite used to seeing wayward human beings drifting purposelessly in and out of her field of peripheral vision. To a cat, all human beings are relegated to the peripheries of life. This is also the way most human beings look at other human beings. Unfortunately, our fields of peripheral vision are not as large or as well developed as those of the cat.

I set fire to a cigar and paced back and forth a bit while the cat watched from her rocking chair. On about my seventh crossing of the dusty wooden floor I noticed something else that was out of place in the loft. The blue down sleeping bag that had been left at camp many years ago by Ryan Kalmin had been folded neatly on the sofa when I'd left for Washington. Not it was unfolded and lying on the floor next to the window by the fire escape.

The significance of the sleeping bag was something that did not escape me, but I wanted to confirm my theory with Rambam, who would still be in hibernation for another forty-three hours or so. Possibly I'd have to call him and cause him to leap sideways. I studied the window by the fire escape again. It did not appear to have been tampered with.

I planned to take Polly Price to Asti's, which was not a particularly quiet place, but what I had to tell her wasn't going to take long. Maybe I'd invite McGovern to join us there a little later as well. Polly said she had wanted to meet him before they took him away to the mental hospital and, judging from his recent messages on my machine, this might be her last chance. Might as well make it one big, unhappy family, I thought, as I reclined upon the sofa for a brief power nap before the evening's entertainment.

Of course, I'd probably want to take a few more of Dr. Fouad's rocket beans before I picked up Polly and we got together with McGovern. Like I always say, if you're going to kill two birds, you might as well get stoned.

Chapter Twenty

The fat lady was already singing by the time Augie had shown Polly and me to our table at Asti's. Of course, the fat lady was always singing at Asti's. Or else somebody was acting out some opera dressed up as a bullfighter. Or playing the cash register and the bottles at the bar along with Eddie on the piano. It was not a particularly quiet or romantic table, but the mood of its two occupants was, alas, far from quiet or romantic. Indeed, somewhere between the time we'd ordered drinks and the time the Asti's Deluxe Antipasto had arrived, Polly and I had set about openly bickering. This did not upset the other diners, who probably thought we were part of the show. It did not, however, serve as a digestive aid for the lavish meal that I knew Augie always provided his patrons.

"What I want to know," said Polly while waiting for her second scotch, "is what happened in Washington, how did you manage to get yourself shot, and what does all this have to do with finding Derrick?" In her blue eyes I could see a chill wind blowing.

"I'll be happy to report it all to you," I said, "but then you have to promise to tell me the truth about something I want to know."

"Agreed," she said, nodding as the waiter brought her scotch. Polly, I noticed, was the kind of woman who would take a drink. Of course, there were circumstances, and, in this case, I suppose I was part of them.

"Not 'agreed,'" I said, pinning her with my best vulnerable-tough-guy look. "I want you to promise you'll tell me the truth about something."

"I promise," she said icily.

"Good," I said. "We should get together socially more often."

"Keep dreaming," she said.

I looked around in the vain hope that McGovern would be arriving earlier than planned. If things continued like this, we were going to need a buffer before our menus arrived and I had to order my client to leave the restaurant.

"There's nothing wrong with dreaming," I said, in the way of small talk. "Lawrence of Arabia spoke of the dangerous men who dream in the daytime."

"If that's what you've been doing," she said, "I want my retainer back."

We bantered in this fashion for a while, as I continued to drink in her good looks, which only seemed to increase with her anger and impatience. I was also killing time, trying to decide exactly what to tell her. Finally, I decided to tell her everything just as it happened. I could only hope that Polly Price would be as forthcoming with me. If not, it was her funeral, I figured. Of course, in light of recent events, it could also be mine.

Between the time we ordered and the time the food arrived, I was able to regurgitate almost everything that had occurred in Washington. While Polly was picking at her salad, I filled her in on the break-in at the loft and the theft of Derrick's papers. Except for a brief moue of something akin to pity, when I described how I'd gotten winged by the cops, Polly seemed to take it all in rather stoically.

"So somebody doesn't want you to find Derrick," she said.

"Or Derrick doesn't want me to find Derrick," I said.

Polly didn't seem to like that idea much, but that was the way the breadstick crumbled. We never are who we think we are and the people we think we know are never the people we think we know and the little country station never stays in one place long enough for us to hear the end of the song. Every time Cinderella marries Rockefeller, here comes Jesse James.

"Which segues nicely into what I want to know. If you're so concerned about finding your husband, why not call the police? The truth, Polly. You promised to tell me the truth."

Polly looked down at her lobster Fra Diavolo. The fat lady was now singing "Happy Talk" from

South Pacific. "*You've got to have a dream . . . If you don't have a dream . . . How you gonna have a dream come true?*"

Polly had a dream, all right. But, as often happens in this grainy old black-and-white world, her dream was turning into somebody else's nightmare. And as I watched a blue teardrop make a tiny little splash into her Chivas, I began to realize that the somebody else was me.

"Derrick's been in trouble before," she said softly. "Some financial discrepancies arose. But some of his partners stepped in and smoothed it over. I didn't think it would happen again. He promised me it wouldn't. Now I don't know what to think. I can't go to the police. Will you still help me find him?"

I took Polly's hand and gave it a little squeeze. Her eyes were the color of bluegrass mountains after the rains.

"Wherever he is and whatever he's done," I said, "I'll help you find him."

Polly squeezed my hand in the heartbreaking manner of a child who now believed that everything was going to be all right.

Then a large man squeezed himself into the chair beside me. It was McGovern, and judging from his rather ebullient demeanor, he'd already had a few of the tall vodka drinks that bore his name.

"Let me guess what happened to your wrist," he said, in a voice loud enough to make a number of nearby tables pause over their pasta. "You were jerkin' off and your balls blew up!"

Chapter Twenty-One

McGovern, however, was not without charm. He'd come into contact with many fascinating people in his life, not the least of which was himself. And now that was part of the problem, I thought: how well he was in contact with himself. I wasn't a psychiatrist and I didn't know. All I knew for sure was that if I were a psychiatrist I probably wouldn't have many patients, because I wouldn't be forever sipping a cup of tea and constantly asking them how something made them feel. I'd be kicking their asses out of my office for feeling sorry for themselves and then reminding them that a kick in the ass can be a big assist in helping them take that first big step forward. Then, after kicking their asses, I'd bill their asses. It sounded like a pretty good racket. Of course, there were people in this world who did need help, no doubt more than I could provide. Unfortunately, at least two of them were sitting at my table.

But they weren't alone. I was having problems of my own at the moment. Cutting a cognac-covered, peppercorned, big, hairy steak with one arm in a sling is harder than Japanese arithmetic. Somehow, I managed. It was heartening to see that McGovern's Irish charm seemed to be working on Polly Price. As he recounted his own troubles in self-effacing, humorous, colorful anecdotes, some of the tension appeared to go out of Polly's well-constructed body. Whereas, moments ago she'd been crying, now she was smiling sympathetically, laughing, and shaking her pretty head in disbelief.

McGovern's intrusion, as well as giving me a chance to eat, also provided me with a little time to digest what Polly had revealed about the check-ered character of her husband. It confirmed the feeling I'd had for some time now that Derrick had been the architect, or one of the architects, of his own disappearance. It didn't mean that Der-rick was out of danger, but it did serve to take a bit of the life-or-death urgency out of the case, maybe buy a little more time for me and possibly shed some light on a few new angles and areas to explore.

Derrick, it now seemed quite clear, was not the good little church worker that Polly had at first described. He obviously had perpetrated some sort of fraud or scam and now, quite possibly, had gotten in over his head. I'd find him, all right, I thought. I just hoped it wouldn't be in the trunk of a rent-a-car at JFK. But at least I now knew pretty damn well what it was I was looking for. That was more than most people could say.

"Tell me more about this Leaning Jesus char-acter," Polly was saying.

"He should've been dead by now," said McGovern. "Of course, so should Kinky."

"So should you," I said a little testily. "We've both just struggled with slightly different demons."

"Leaning Jesus?" said Polly, like a small child asking if you'd brought her something.

"That's why I wanted to talk to Lord Peter Wimsey here," said McGovern. "I've gotten three more calls from Leaning Jesus since you left town."

"According to your chronology," I said, "he's got to be about a hundred and seven years old."

"Not really. I met him when I was sixteen. A mere slip of a lad. He taught me how to cook, how to play Hollywood gin, and he introduced me to an older woman who taught me the ways of the world."

"You've still got a lot to learn, McGovern," I said, already growing bored with the conversation. Polly, however, was hooked.

"And he really was Al Capone's personal chef?" she asked.

"I suspect he probably had some other duties, as well," said McGovern. "But that's how I knew him." McGovern conferred with a waiter and, magically, a Vodka McGovern soon materialized before him.

"Did you ever meet Capone?" Polly wanted to know.

"No. In nineteen thirty-two, Capone went to prison for eleven years, the last nine he served in Alcatraz. When he got out he went to his estate on Palm Island, Florida, where he died in nineteen forty-seven. So he was a little before my time."

"Just a *little* before your time," I said.

"Anyway, I was only sixteen and Leaning Jesus seemed like an old man to me, but he could've been younger. It's possible he's still alive and in his mid-eighties."

"It's possible," I said, "that these calls are emanating from the area code of Jupiter. What does he say when he calls? 'Hi. I'm Leaning Jesus and you may be the next recipient of big prizes from the Publishers Clearing House'?"

"Stop, Kinky," said Polly, already siding with McGovern. "Let Mike tell us what he said."

"Well," said McGovern, finishing his drink and warming up to the feminine interest, "it's really strange. The last call sounded angry. Kind of threatening in a way."

"What'd he say?" I asked, beginning to feel a little uneasy in spite of the ridiculous nature of the situation.

"He said: 'You've got it. I know you've got it. Give it up, kid.'"

McGovern had recited Leaning Jesus's words in his own version of an old mobster's voice. Polly had listened in rapt attention. Then she'd shivered slightly.

"Okay, McGovern," I said, "let's assume for the sake of argument that Leaning Jesus really is calling you. What the hell could you possibly have that he wants?"

"I don't know," said McGovern. "I just know what *I* want."

"What?" asked Polly.

"Another Vodka McGovern," he said.

Chapter Twenty-Two

In 1953, when I was about seven years old, my parents took me to see Shoshone the Magic Pony. That was also the year that Tom and Min Friedman bought Echo Hill Ranch and turned it into a children's camp, providing thousands of boys and girls with many happy, carefree summers of fun. Echo Hill also provided the setting for one of my more successful cases, recorded in *Armadillos & Old Lace*. But although 1953 might've been a good year for the Friedmans and a good year for wine, it'd been a bad year for almost everybody and everything else. Hank Williams, along with Julius and Ethel Rosenberg, had checked out of the mortal motel that year, quite possibly unaware that the other party had been there to begin with. Hank fried his brains and heart and other internal organs for our sins, using eleven different kinds of herbs and spices. Julius and Ethel, charged with spying for Russia, many thought falsely, were fried by our government and died declaring their innocence and their love for each other. Hank's songs declared his innocence and his love, inexplicably, for people. It is doubtful whether Hank and the Rosenbergs had anything in common at all, except that a small boy in Texas had cried when each of them died.

The boy had also cried the year before when Adlai Stevenson had lost the potato-sack hop at the company picnic to good ol' Ike, the Garth Brooks of all presidents, who turned out to be the most significant leader we'd had since Millard Fillmore and remained as popular as the bottle of ketchup on the kitchen table of America, even if Lenny Bruce and Judy Garland, who were destined to both die on toilets, like Elvis, remained in their rooms for the entire two terms of his presidency.

The kid had seemed to cry a bit back then, but fortunately, human tragedies of this sort never cut into his happy childhood. When he grew up, he continued to cry at times, though the tears were no longer visible in or to the naked eye, for he never let human tragedies of this sort cut into his cocktail hour. But during his childhood, it is very likely that his parents noticed the tears. That may have been the reason they took him to see Shoshone the Magic Pony.

Now, on a gray afternoon, on the day following the dinner at Asti's, I found myself looking out over Vandam Street and dreaming in the daytime like Lawrence of Arabia. I could afford to dream in the daytime, I thought. Last night had gone well with Polly, and it didn't even bother me when she and McGovern exchanged phone numbers and hobbies, thereby slightly enlarging their own support groups, while mine continued, almost inexorably, to atrophy. I wasn't jealous of Polly's apparent fascination with my favorite Irish poet. Not yet.

I'd also gotten through to Rambam finally and was expecting him to drop by sometime this afternoon. There were things he could be very helpful with, I felt, pertaining to the whereabouts of one Derrick Price. And, if there was any time left over, maybe I'd take a whirl at straightening out Leaning Jesus.

I looked out over the cold, listless afternoon, and my mind went back again to the summertime of 1953. Shoshone the Magic Pony had just been announced over the loud speaker at the little rodeo arena near Bandera, Texas. My father and mother, Tom and Min, were sitting on the splintery wooden bleachers next to me and my little brother, Roger. And suddenly, all our eyes were on the center of the arena.

Shoshone came out prancing, led by an old cowboy with a big beard. He took the reins and bridle off Shoshone and the horse bowed several times to the audience. Shoshone had a beautiful saddle and a large saddle blanket that seemed to glitter with sequins of red, white, and blue. Then the old cowboy stood back and the music began. It was "The Tennessee Waltz." And Shoshone the Magic Pony started to dance.

It was apparent from the outset, even to us children in the crowd, that there were two men inside the body of Shoshone. You could tell by the clever, intricate soft-shoe routine she was performing, by the fact that she often appeared to be moving hilariously in two directions at once, and by the funny and very unponylike way she now and again humped and arched her back to the music. I was laughing so hard I forgot for the moment about Hank Williams, Adlai Stevenson, the Rosenbergs, and myself. Whoever was inside there was so good, I even forgot that they were inside there.

Then "The Tennessee Waltz" was over.

Shoshone bowed a deep, theatrical bow. Everybody laughed and clapped and cheered. The old cowboy took off his hat. Then he took off his beard. Then he took off the old cowboy mask he was wearing and we saw to our amazement that the old-timer was in reality a very pretty young girl.

She took off Shoshone's saddle. Then she took off her saddle blanket. And there, to my total astonishment, stood only Shoshone the Magic Pony.

Shoshone was a real horse.

"And so you see," I said to the cat, who during my childhood reflections had been gazing at her own reflection on the windowpane, "there is a lesson in all this."

The cat did not seem to see the lesson. She was so self-absorbed that all she appeared to care about was her reflection. I plodded on.

"The lesson," I said, "is that nothing is what it appears to be. And no one is *who* they appear to be. It can be a rather useful spiritual tool for private investigators, people in general, and some cats."

At almost precisely that moment, there came a soul-wrenching, rather primitive, vaguely Palestinian keening noise from somewhere on the street below. I looked down to observe that Rambam had parked his car on the sidewalk and was standing there with one hand lifted in what appeared

88

to be a somewhat arcane gesture of somewhat intense Middle-Eastern obscenity. I opened the window.

"I'm freezing my ass off down here!" he shouted. "Throw down that fuckin' puppet head!"

"And sometimes," I said to the cat, as I walked over to the refrigerator, "a Rambam is simply a Rambam."

Chapter Twenty-Three

A short while later, Rambam and I were sitting at the kitchen table drinking espresso. The cat was sitting on the kitchen table watching Rambam drink espresso. I had to admit that it did look rather ridiculous for a big, tough guy like Rambam to be drinking from such a dainty little thimble, but it was one of the few gifts I'd received from friendly, misguided gentiles that year and I was determined to use it for something besides housing dead cockroaches.

"Don't you have something to drink from besides this little fucking demitasse?" said Rambam, always the gracious guest.

"The Dowager Duchess of New Jersey found it quite lovely," I said. "Stephanie DuPont gave it to me before she left for St. Moritz. Would you care to see the whole set?"

"Not really," said Rambam, "but you could always break it out if you have the Gay Men's Choir of Manhattan as your next client."

"How about I pour some espresso in the bull's horn? It's a rare privilege to drink from the Kinkster's bull's horn."

"Don't you have a goddamn coffee cup in the

house?"

"Not that you would enjoy drinking from. They're all being used for laboratory experiments by Alexander Fleming. The only functioning coffee cup in the loft is the one I'm drinking from, my official Imus in the Morning coffee mug. And it's not in particularly great shape."

"Neither is Imus," said Rambam, getting up to refill his demitasse.

"The I-Man's doing all right," I said. "He's hauling down about eight mil a year, he's got a beautiful new wife who's about ninety-seven years younger than him, and he's got a huge country estate in Southport."

"But he doesn't have a little black puppet head," said Rambam, standing by the refrigerator and patting the puppet head several times, a little harder than necessary. "Which reminds me, why don't *you* move somewhere a bit more upscale? Say, anyplace that doesn't directly abut the city's main garbage truck depot?"

"And they still don't pick up the garbage."

"I noticed," said Rambam, getting up again rather irritably to refill his demitasse.

I sat back and lit a cigar and thought about how best to handle Rambam. All I'd told him on the phone was that I'd gotten a new client and a hefty retainer, that I was looking for a missing husband, and that I'd already managed to get myself winged by a cop in our nation's capital. He was a working PI, and this was not his case. I didn't want to take advantage of his friendship. I just wanted to pick his brains thoroughly enough so that somebody wouldn't blow away mine.

Thus it was that two cigars later, with Rambam having jumped up intermittently and, at least to

me, quite entertainingly, to refill his demitasse, I'd told him the whole story. He'd made a number of rather insightful observations already. One had been to stop the next time a cop yelled "Freeze!" or I might get a warning shot right between the eyes. Another had been that the wayward sleeping bag had probably been placed over the windowsill during the break-in to avoid leaving evidence and indicated a rather surprisingly sophisticated job. Another one was something I'd already figured out for myself. That the setup in Washington and the break-in in New York had occurred in basically the same time frame and might indicate that I was up against some kind of large outfit.

"But how did they even know that Polly had hired me?" I said.

"She's your basic woman client. She probably told her best friend and *she* told *her* best friend and the next thing you know you've got a sleeping bag over your windowsill and a bullet through your arm. How is your arm, by the way?"

"I'll be able to play," I said.

"You'd better be careful. Whoever these guys are, they seem to be going to a lot of trouble to stop you."

"You think Derrick's alive, then?"

"Until they leave his dead body on your doorstep, assume that he is."

"Maybe they're waiting for Derrick to strike oil," I said, "and then they'll cap him."

Rambam laughed very briefly. More of a bark, really. From a dog you didn't want chasing you.

"I'll do some checking for you," said Rambam. "How the cops showed up so fast in Washington. And how somebody could afford to lose that much

91

cocaine. It does suggest some possibilities and none of them are good. In the meantime, you should sit tight. It's safer for you, and besides, I don't really see any active leads for you to follow."

"There's got to be something I can do."

"You can practice masturbating with your left hand," said Rambam, as he headed for the door.

"I'm afraid that's impossible," I said to his large, retreating back. "My penis sloughed off when I was working with the Peace Corps in the jungles of Borneo."

"That would explain a lot of things."

"Well, before you leave, I'd like you to explain one thing to me. What do I do about McGovern and this Leaning Jesus business?"

"You follow the number-one rule of all good private investigators: Don't work for clients without a fee."

"Yeah, but do you think there's anything to it?"

"I don't know," said Rambam, as he opened the door. "Sometimes even paranoids have real enemies."

Chapter Twenty-Four

"That's a good bit of deductive reasoning on Rambam's part," I said to the cat by way of explanation. "He knows I'm left-handed. He knows I've injured my right arm. He knows if you bat left you masturbate right. And vice versa. That's why he said I should practice masturbating with my left hand."

The cat appeared to be appalled by my rather lascivious sermonette.

"Don't worry," I said. "I'm not going to indulge

in self-gratification with my left hand. Not even to fantasies of Polly Price. Do you know why?"

The cat did not appear to know why. I wasn't sure I knew why either. Spanking my simian seemed like a fairly appropriate action at this stage of the game.

"Look, it's not such a big deal in the whole spiritual scheme of things. Say I break two of the top ten commandments. I cast my seed upon my loft. And I covet my client's ass. What's the worst thing that can happen? God'll ground me?"

The cat was rapidly losing interest in the subject and, quite frankly, so was I. I walked over and shook hands with the Jameson bottle and poured a long shot into the bull's horn. The whole damn thing's a long shot, I thought. How am I going to find this bastard with such a large, Hydra-headed force field of evil arrayed against me and this bastard I'm looking for is part of it?

I remembered something my father had once told me. It was something to the effect that a person can be characterized by the size of the enemies he fights. Small battles are indicative of a petty mind. Large battles are in keeping with being possessed of a big spirit. My father, I recalled, had two rather unusual heroes of the last half of the twentieth century: Natan Sharansky and Rosa Parks. According to my father, they both took on the system and they both beat the system and they're both still alive. I toasted my father for being the kind of man who could have two heroes like Natan Sharansky and Rosa Parks. Then I poured the shot down my neck.

The cat, like many Americans, probably had never heard of Natan Sharansky, but as far as I was concerned, they could all look it up when they got home. Ask the man at the Greyhound station. Of course, I had my own two heroes of the twentieth century. Hank Williams, the Hillbilly Shakespeare, and Anne Frank, the Jewish Joan of Arc. They didn't take on the system, they didn't beat the system, and they were both dead. What the hell. Different windmill strokes, I suppose.

I set fire to a cigar and went over to the little table where my unused chess set stood waiting in dust and cobwebs to be touched by the hand of man or God. I sat down and studied the board. Patterns are always interesting even if they're not there yet. I filled the bull's horn again and tried to remember something Polly Price had said that had vaguely bothered me at the time. I couldn't remember. It would come to me. I looked at the chess pieces and they looked at me and it started to get darker outside. I meditated on the board for a while, thinking of the legendary game Abraham Lincoln once played with a rather saturnine Supreme Court justice. As they played, Abe's young son, Tad, kept pestering his father for attention. This did not faze Abe but irritated the judge enormously. Abe smoked his pipe and told Tad to pull his lips together and he'd be right with him after the game. But Tad, in childish anger, at last reacted by suddenly sweeping all the pieces off the board. This action caused the Supreme Court justice to become highly agitato. Abe, however, calmly continued to smoke his pipe and study the empty board as if he was still searching for his next move. Finally, Lincoln stood up and looked across at the apoplectic old judge. "That's Tad's game," he said.

But this wasn't Tad's game, I thought. It wasn't Rambam's. It wasn't even Polly Price's anymore.

It was my game to win.

I was still staring at the board when the phones began ringing. I got up and ankled it over to the desk and collared the blower on the left.

"Family counseling services," I said.

"Kinkstah!" said a familiar, rodentlike voice.

It was Ratso. Not Washington. New York.

"Kinkstah!" said the voice again, several decibels louder. "I got to talk to you."

"Okay, Rat. Start talkin'."

"I just got a very strange phone call from somebody named Leaning Jesus."

Chapter Twenty-Five

This was exactly what I didn't want to happen. To become sidetracked. To lose focus. To get caught up in the sideshow. To forget what side my bread was buttered on. To use a large number of clichés. But in light of the fact that the search for Derrick Price had virtually slogged to a standstill, this appeared to be as good a time as any to become sidetracked. Rambam was right. The Price missing person investigation was *the* case. But if I encountered any significant dead time, pardon the expression, I might as well follow out a lead for McGovern. It was at least as efficient a use of time and energy as talking to a cat or playing chess with Tad Lincoln.

I waited for Ratso out on Mott Street that evening, smoking a cigar and making small talk, no pun intended, with the Chinese dwarf who used the same corner to paint pastels on a makeshift easel. The guy was very good, now that I, unlike millions of other people in the city, had at last slowed down to notice. Might even be the Toulouse-Lautrec of Chinatown. I'd buy some of his work sometime, I figured. Of course, the only art that I'd managed to collect so far in my life was my pre-Columbian cat-turd collection, which I still had high hopes for. On the other hand, diversification into Chinese-dwarf pastels might make a rather sound investment. I was still weighing the possibilities when I heard a macawlike voice calling from somewhere up the street.

"Kinkstah! Let's go, baby! Kinkstah! Big Wong's!"

It was Ratso, and it didn't take me long to realize that rumors of his sartorial improvement had been greatly exaggerated. He still looked pretty much like Ratso. Pink trousers with Elvis Presley song titles scrawled all over them in hot purple. Unfashionable and unpleasant-looking raccoon coat and coonskin cap with the creature's head attached, eyes sewn shut. Antique red shoes which, I knew from past experience, had once resided on the wheels of a man who had gone to Jesus. The only new affectations, in fact, that would seem to indicate an impending influx of bucks, were an expensive-looking Burberry scarf and a cigar that I now noticed was a very nice torpedo-shaped Habana Montecristo No. 2.

"Kinkstah!" said Ratso again, like some form of annoying modern urban mantra. "Kinkstah!"

"I see you've upgraded your taste in cigars," I said, as we walked up Mott Street toward Big Wong's.

"Yeah. These are top-drawer. Sorry I don't have another one to give you. My lawyer got this out of a special humidor that was given to him by a former client."

"I'm glad to see they're good for something."

"Humidors?"

"No," I said. "Lawyers."

It was almost like old times as Ratso and I walked into Big Wong's together. It wasn't clear whether there was any truth to Tom Baker's theory that the waiters thought I was a Mafia don because I tipped so extravagantly. Ted Mann's notion that the waiters regarded Ratso and myself as two friendly homosexuals because we'd never come in the place with a broad was also a possibility. Whatever their motivation, the waiters and busboys dropped whatever they were doing and came forth to greet the two of us like long-lost brothers.

"Oooh-lah-lah! Ooooh-lah-lah!" Ratso and I offered as part of the intercultural mating call.

"Kee-kee! Chee-chee!" shouted the waiters in return.

Other diners, almost all of them of the Oriental persuasion, looked up briefly, with maddeningly inscrutable expressions. Then, just as quickly, they returned their attention to their pork gruel. Ted Mann's addendum to his theory was that "Kee-kee" and "Chee-chee" meant "crazy" and "smelly" in Mandarin. From the reaction of the house tonight, this could not be ruled out as a possibility either.

"Kee-kee," said the waiter, as he placed a glass of hot tea in front of me. "Chee-chee," he said, as he performed the same action for Ratso.

"Kee-kee," I said, "is obviously a bastardization of Kinky."

"If that's the case, where does 'Chee-chee' come from?"

"Lower Baboon's Asshole," I said. "For the

present, how about telling me about that phone call you got from Leaning Jesus?"

Ratso quickly looked at his menu in a vain effort to hide a mischievous little smile. I knew at once that there'd been no Leaning Jesus phone call to Ratso. Surprisingly, I was not even angry about his little prank. I took it rather philosophically. It was a small disappointment, I reflected, in a lifetime of disappointments.

"So you've been talking to McGovern?" I said.

"That's right, Sherlock. And I've evolved a little theory that's quite fascinating."

"Let others be the judge of that," I said curtly.

The waiter took our orders. I ordered the soy sauce chicken chopped Chinese style and a bowl of wonton mein soup, the best soup in the world, I had to admit, including the matzo-ball soup at the Carnegie Deli. Ratso was enormously disappointed to learn that the restaurant had run out of roast pork. He took it well, however, and made do with three other dishes, including the ever-popular squid with sour Chinese vegetables.

"This is a classic case," Ratso said, before the waiter had even turned his back, "of MIBs."

"MIBs?"

"You know. MIBs. Men in black. The otherworldly creatures that always appear in the life of anyone in the weeks after they claim to have seen a UFO. It's all in John Keel's book, *The Mothman Prophecies.*"

I remembered the book vaguely. What I remembered most about it was that it had scared the hell out of me at the time. It was not a work of fiction. Keel, who was a rather eccentric, scholarly friend of Ratso's, had painstakingly chronicled the subsequent almost invariable deterioration that had occurred in the lives of people who had reported seeing UFOs. Fortunately, he did not record the deterioration that had occurred in the lives of those of us who have not seen UFOs.

"It all fits," Ratso was saying. "By the way, you seem to be favoring your right arm. You didn't get hit by another tranquilizer dart like that time at Madison Square Garden, did you?"

"No, I was—uh—jerkin' off and my balls blew up." Ratso might, indeed, be helpful with the McGovern matter, but the charming naïveté that he occasionally lent to a case was not going to help plunge the plugged-up commode that was also known as the Derrick Price investigation.

"Common household accident," Ratso was going on. "You're sure you weren't trying to hang yourself while you were spanking your monkey? Autoerotic death syndrome is quite common among teenagers these days."

"Not common enough," I said grimly. "Back to McGovern."

"It all fits," Ratso said again. "McGovern sees a little green man. Then electronic devices start fucking up in his house. The television turns on and off mysteriously. The telephone starts disconnecting, echoing, clanging, beeping. The blender turns on by itself—"

"Hold the weddin'. He never told me about the blender."

"Yes, the blender, the television, the telephone. These are classic electronic interruptions that always occur after the subject sees a UFO, according to Keel. Of course, if you're a cynic you could also say there's probably some loose wiring in McGovern's apartment."

"Or you could say there's probably some loose

wiring in McGovern's brain."

At this point, the waiter arrived with the food. Ratso paused briefly to order duck sauce, ginger sauce, soy sauce, and hot red oil chili sauce. I thought about what the great frog philosopher Voltaire said about the British: "The English have 365 different religions and only one sauce." Then I thought about the H.P. Sauce that McGovern had railed against at Myers of Keswick. Then I thought about McGovern. Then Ratso was talking again, this time with his mouth partially full of squid and sour Chinese vegetables.

"According to John Keel, the men in black, or MIBs, who may be from the government or may be supernatural creatures, begin to appear shortly after these electronic phenomena occur. The MIBs are often said to wear clothing that's decades out of fashion."

"Much like yourself."

"No. Their clothes are new and they frequently are seen to drive mint-condition Cadillacs from the fifties and sixties with their headlights off at night."

"New Jersey plates?"

"You can poke fun at it all you want, but Keel has interviewed thousands of people who've reported close encounters, and McGovern fits the profile perfectly. The guy he claims he saw on his fire escape sounds a hell of a lot like a typical MIB. The little supernatural trick of a dry wallet left outside a locked window in the rain also fits perfectly."

"So does a drunken McGovern losing his wallet on the fire escape."

"But the wallet was dry."

"So's the soy sauce chicken."

"Then you've got the paranoia factor. McGovern thinks he's being followed, thinks he's being spied upon. No one believes him. Not even some of his best friends." Here Ratso stopped his chopsticks in midair to eye me coolly. I met his gaze, then returned to slurping my wonton soup.

"Don't you see, Sherlock? Not everything can be explained by deductive reasoning. McGovern's like the high school football coach Keel interviewed in Alabama. Crew cut redneck, total cracker. An average Joe until he makes a sighting. Then come the electronic phenomena, the men in black, the paranoia, the disbelief of friends and family, the disruption of normal life, the obsession with the situation, the divorce, the alcoholism, and before long you have—"

"—the typical American?"

We finished the meal in thankful silence. Obviously, McGovern had done quite a fair bit of yapping to Ratso about his situation. There was nothing wrong with that, I thought. Ratso was a friend, McGovern needed friends, we all needed friends. McGovern already believed an old man with a turban was following him around. What further harm could Ratso cause by getting involved? Meanwhile, maybe McGovern would leave me alone long enough for me to justify the confidence Polly Price had placed in me.

Eventually, the waiter returned to drop the hatchet. Ratso made a feint or two for his wallet but I ended up paying the check and leaving an extravagant tip because I wanted people to like me. It didn't always work.

Ratso hadn't mentioned his impending inheritance, so I assumed it was still impending. I hadn't mentioned the bill he still owed me for services rendered. He'd pay me one of these days. I'd find true love. I'd live happily ever after. The world would be at peace. Big Wong's would continue to be a killer-bee restaurant until some nerd from *The New York Times* walked in with a bow tie and an umbrella and wrote the place up and gave it a couple of stars and soon they'd be serving sweet-and-sour veal and giving fortune cookies and nobody'd ever say Kee-kee or Chee-chee again.

When I got back to the loft that night there were three messages on my answering machine that torpedoed my little sabbatical from crime solving and caused me to become highly agitato. The first was from McGovern, who'd just had a visit from two men all dressed in black. The second message was from Polly Price, who'd just found a message on her answering machine confirming Derrick Price's meeting the next day in Chicago at Merrill Lynch to "prepare trust documents." The third message was from Rambam. It was, like Rambam, rather terse and to the point. Derrick Price's automobile registration papers had expired seven years ago. And so, according to Rambam, had Derrick Price.

I took a fresh cigar out of Sherlock Holmes's porcelain head. I studied it thoughtfully for a moment, then lit a kitchen match and set fire to the end of it. I puffed until it glowed like a gypsy campfire in the distance. Then I got up and walked over to the counter and stroked the cat.

"It's time," I said, "to reach out and touch somebody."

The cat, of course, said nothing.

Chapter Twenty-Six

As the big jet vectored tediously above O'Hare Airport, many loose thoughts vectored equally tediously around my somewhat frazzled mind. I'd chosen not to tell Polly Price yet about Rambam's discovery that her loving husband had been dead for seven years. That kind of sudden news can be hard on a wife. Besides, Rambam was hardly infallible and I never did much believe in computers. Also, somebody thought Derrick Price was supposed to be at a meeting that would be taking place very shortly at Merrill Lynch to prepare trust documents. That sounded like a euphemism for stashing some of the money Price may have been routing through Roscoe West and Associates in our nation's capital. If I could catch Price at that meeting it would be living proof that he wasn't dead. If this plane ever landed at O'Hare, it would be living proof that I wasn't dead.

As we continued to turn and circle over the Windy City, I stared out the window into the gray, viscous soup that provided such an apt metaphor for the direction, or lack of it, the case was taking. Why, I asked myself, was this flight different from all other flights? Why was I going to Chicago if Derrick Price was dead? The answer was that I had what we big private dicks called a hunch and fortunately for me it wasn't on my back. This, I believed, was one of the rare occasions when Rambam and his hard-boiled computer were wrong.

My decision to come to Chicago had been so sperm of the moment that I hadn't even told my client. When Polly had informed me about the message regarding Derrick's meeting, I'd left her with the impression that I planned to sit on my buttocks and take it under advisement. I did not share Rambam's male-chauvinist view that a female client always tells her best friend who tells *her* best friend who tells *her* best friend and you wind up having to vigorously employ your getaway sticks to avoid being set up with half of Peru. It was much more likely, I reflected, as I gazed out into the unnerving, unending goo, that my own barrage of telephone calls had stirred up the nest of yellowjackets. Getting winged once a week was about all I could handle, so I'd made no advance calls to Chicago.

"Can you see anything yet?" asked the woman on the aisle seat as she nervously fingered a cross that was big enough to drown a horse.

"I can see we're in for a rather unpleasant experience," I said. If anything, the gray goo was getting thicker outside the window.

"You can't see *anything* down there?" she asked again, her rather hirsute upper lip breaking out in a sweat.

"Wait a minute," I said, with my eyeballs aimed downward as close to the window as my hat would allow. "I thought we were passing over the River Jordan, but I guess it's just a cloud formation."

"Folks," said the pilot over the intercom. Then he paused and all of my fellow passengers to the grave waited on the edge of panic. It's always a bad sign when a pilot pauses after "Folks."

"It looks like traffic is heavy into O'Hare," he continued after a brief eternity. "The tower hopes to give us landing clearance in about thirty minutes—"

A collective groan went up. It seemed not dissimilar to the sound you might have heard if all the air had suddenly gone out of God's basketball. Kind of like the sound the crowd makes at a Rolling Stones concert when Mick Jagger announces they're going to perform a new song.

Now some turbulence began to inject itself into the little equation and this had the rather disheartening effect of provoking the lady next to me into dragging out her Bible and murmuring madly to her Lord. I wasn't sure where my Lord was at the moment. Maybe He was sitting in the Carnegie Deli eating a salami sandwich. Maybe He'd gone to the country for the weekend.

Only two Americans knew where I was. To get my mind off the present tedium, I thought about them now. Rambam had been against my coming to Chicago. He'd wanted more time to run down information on Derrick Price. Whether Price was alive or dead, he felt I should approach the Merrill Lynch meeting with great care. If a party professing to be Price showed up, something was definitely going on, Rambam felt, that was not in your kosher area. On the other hand, why would the nonspiritual corporate denizens of Merrill Lynch want to hold a seance for a dead guy? Obviously, others beside myself believed Price was still lurking around somewhere along this mortal coil. How I was going to get into the meeting was another problem, but I could deal with it once we landed. I hoped that would be soon, because the lady on the aisle was now holding her cross up to me and talking in tongues.

The other American who knew my whereabouts was McGovern. Unlike Rambam, he'd been very excited about my rather abrupt plans to go to Chicago. He'd hoped that after I'd located Polly Price's wayward husband I'd be able to take a little time to lean on Leaning Jesus.

Suddenly, we heard the thump of the landing gear coming down and locking in. The lady on the aisle looked up from her Bible in shock.

"What was that?" she demanded.

"Can't see a thing," I said. "Maybe we just T-boned a band of angels."

"Lord help us!" shouted the lady.

"Amen to that," I said conversationally.

It was quite an unusual case, I thought to myself. It was quite an unusual client-investigator relationship. There was no way to round up the usual suspects. There weren't any. There was only the shadow man, Derrick Price.

Just as I was thinking these dark thoughts, the plane descended through the last layer of the soup that so long had surrounded us. And for the first time in what seemed like weeks, I thought I could see the light of day.

Chapter Twenty-Seven

The Merrill Lynch offices were located in downtown Chicago just inside the Loop and very near the area where Abbie Hoffman led his Yippie Charge of the Light Brigade against the Chicago police in 1968. I was eating monkey brains with the pygmies in the jungles of Borneo at the time, so I missed out on the action in that particular theater of the war. I didn't meet Abbie until some years later at the Chelsea Hotel in New York in room 1010, Janis Joplin's old room. It was while Abbie was underground and on the run from the feds that I first really became his friend. It was after he died like a disillusioned Jewish dinosaur that I realized how very little people truly ever change. Mankind plods on from millennium to millennium in a cruel, pathetic, often stultifyingly dull Bataan Death March of the ages. Not that people don't try. It's just that you walk for thousands of years toward what you think is a beacon of light and when you get there, it's only Joan of Arc with her hair on fire.

I stepped out of the hack on Michigan Avenue and looked at my watch like any good little constipated, humorless law partner on his way back from Bennigan's. It was two-thirty. The much-awaited Derrick Price meeting was at three. Always nice to be punctual, I thought, as I set down my leather Australian bookie's bag on the sidewalk next to the shivering skeletal remains of a man selling pencils.

"Sooner or later," he said, "you're gonna need a pencil."

"I see your point," I said, as I took a pencil from his coffee can and stuffed in a double sawski. I hoped God was watching.

I shouldered the bookie's bag and ankled it up Michigan, lighting a cigar and looking for the right skyscraper. I was traveling light in the dead of winter, but not as light as the guy selling pencils. All I had in the bookie's bag was a box of cigars, one change of clothes, and a hand-tooled toilet kit that I'd picked up twenty years ago in Juarez. You never know when you might have to leave town in a hurry.

I found the address on Michigan Avenue, boot-legged the cigar past building security, and located the Merrill Lynch offices on the building directory. At the bank of elevators I watched one particular Otis box spit out a large assemblage of the species and, quite miraculously, stand empty for a moment. I hopped in, pushed thirty-three, watched the doors close, and headed for the heavens. It was kind of a lonely ride and I found myself singing a line from an old Flying Burrito Brothers song: "On the thirty-third floor, a gold-plated door won't keep out the Lord's burning rain . . ."

It wasn't going to keep me out either. By the time I descended back into the bowels of the city, I planned to be packing a few more pieces to the puzzle that was Derrick Price. If Price was here in person, of course, I could strike the tent and my one-man caravan could wing its way back to New York in triumph, suffering only a mixed metaphor and a few mixed emotions. I had to admit that I'd be surprised and probably a little disappointed if I nailed Price at this meeting and he turned out to be some run-of-the-mill white-collar criminal. The truth was, I wanted more. After what had happened in Washington and the burglary of my loft, I felt I deserved more. On the other hand, finding a missing person is finding a missing person. Or, as they say in Hollywood, a lay's a lay.

I puffed the cigar peacefully on the empty elevator and pondered Rambam's notion that Price was dead. If that were the case, there was a Derrick Price impersonator at work and he was doing a pretty damn good job. But now, with a misguided confirmation call from a colleague, he might finally have tripped himself up. Whoever the hell he was. Identities, according to Rambam, were fairly easy things to create if you were methodical and spread a little money around. There's McNerd's car. There's McNerd's office. There's McNerd's company. There must be a McNerd.

But quite often there isn't. Of course, in those cases you don't usually encounter a Mrs. McNerd.

The doors opened before I got any further with the idea. There wasn't an elevator boy to say "Nice ride" to, so I legged it out into the hallway just as a young, upwardly-mobile couple got in to go down. They immediately popped back out of the elevator with the woman making exaggerated fanning gestures in front of her beak.

"That's beautiful, man," the guy hollered down the hallway at me. "That's beautiful."

I just kept walking. There was no point in getting my bowels in a twist over the matter. They'd just have to wait awhile and then they'd find another elevator. People like that always do.

The receptionist at Merrill Lynch looked up from her space console long enough to give me the fish-eye.

"Can I help you?" she said.

"I'm here for—"

"There's no smoking in the building."

"There's no ashtrays in the building either," I said, looking around at the plushly antiseptic ambience.

"You'll have to leave with that cigar," she said, obviously enjoying the chance to exercise what little authority she had.

"I'll be right back," I said needlessly. The woman's focus was clearly on my leaving. She did not care a fig whether I returned or merely jumped down an open elevator shaft. She did not care if the entire corporate holdings of Merrill Lynch came crashing down on the world market. All she wanted out of life was for a man with a large hat to take his cigar out of the reception area immediately. It was sad, really.

I walked out into the hallway like a biblical leper looking for an empty cave. There were no ashtrays. No one had ever been crazy enough to smoke a cigar in the building before and no accommodation had been made for that unlikely circumstance. So I killed the cigar as best I could with the heel of my boot on the marble floor of the hallway. It lay there like a steaming turd. I walked back into the reception area with renewed determination.

"Can I *help* you," said the receptionist, not bothering to conceal her irritation.

"Yes, little lady," I said, affecting a somewhat more forceful Texas accent. "I'm Billy Bob Bullock, the lawyer from Dallas. I'm up here for the Derrick Price meetin'."

"The what?"

"Derrick Price meetin'. Three o'clock. Would've been here earlier but they wouldn't let my horse into the parkin' garage. Heyeugh-heyeugh-heyeugh!"

"Take a seat, please. I'll call Mr. Beadleheit."

There were lots of couches and lots of glass tables and lots of financial and investment-oriented magazines. You could just sit there and browse forever and after a while that's what I thought was going to happen to me. Then Mr. Beadleheit walked in.

"I'm Mr Beadleheit, the assistant office manager."

"Billy Bob Bullock. Come up from Dallas."

"How nice. How can we help you, Mr. Bullock?"

"I'm here for the Derrick Price meetin' at three o'clock. Should be about now unless my watch is slow."

"There is no Derrick Price meeting scheduled for three o'clock. There is no Derrick Price meeting scheduled for any time. Brenda, do you have a Derrick Price on our client list?"

The receptionist consulted her computer briefly, then looked up and smiled.

"No Derrick Price," she said cheerfully. "In fact, no one named Price at all."

"Mr. Price is not known to us," said Beadleheit.

"Well, I'm a one-legged man at a butt-kickin' contest," I said.

I walked out of the reception area and down the hallway to the elevators feeling almost as stupid as Billy Bob Bullock. I wasn't totally surprised, however. In this business if you don't feel stupid a lot of the time you're not very smart.

Rambam was right, I thought, as I hurtled thirty-three stories downward in the elevator. Everybody was right but me. Either Derrick Price no longer existed or he'd somehow vanished completely from the face of the earth. The trip to Chicago had been a waste of time. My whole life had been a waste of time.

When I stepped out onto the freezing sidewalk of Michigan Avenue, the first thing I did was fish out a fresh cigar and fire it up. I had just raised my head and was starting to puff rather stoically on the stogie when I noticed a shiny black limo parked just to the left of the main entrance to the building. A uniformed driver was standing next to the limo on the sidewalk looking mildly bored and holding up a little sign.

I took a few more patient puffs on the cigar and walked a little closer. Maybe, I thought, my whole life had not been a waste of time.

The sign read: DERRICK PRICE.

Chapter Twenty-Eight

It is a rather tedious fact of life that most of us who are confined to the human condition spend a great deal of time wishing to be something we're not. Or someone we're not. The proctologist, scrupulously washing his hands before and after each patient, dreams of being Dr. Albert Schweitzer. The rock star, as he worries whether to leave the Porsche with valet parking, dreams of saving the rain forest. The bank teller dreams of embezzling a million dollars and moving to Costa Rica. The average Costa Rican dreams of moving to Akron, Ohio, and becoming a bank teller. The many people who lead anonymous little lives long for fame. The handful of people who've become truly trapped in the thing that fame is, invariably long for anonymity. As far as the rest of us go, we have to deal with so many assholes every day we figure we probably should've been proctologists and at least get paid for it.

"I'm Derrick Price," I said to the limo driver.

"Your office has given me your itinerary, sir," said the chauffeur, touching his cap. "I'm to take you to your next meeting, then back to your hotel."

"Sounds fine," I said. "One of these days my office is going to tell me where I'm going."

The limo driver chuckled politely. Then he stepped over to the back door and opened it for me. Somebody was conning somebody here and I might as well find out if it was me. Besides, there's very few chances in life to walk in another man's shoes, unless, of course, you're Ratso and your closet floor is covered with other men's shoes, the owners of which have previously gone to Jesus.

I got into the limo.

The driver smiled and shut the door, reassuringly touching his cap again. As he walked around to the driver's side door, I settled back for the ride. I wondered briefly how I was able to do what I was apparently doing. It was a bit like voluntarily flying off with the extraterrestrial crew of a UFO, and it isn't always courage that enables you to proceed with that kind of mission. It is often only a rather heady mix of stubbornness and maybe something else, I thought: a little thing called emptiness. The Plexiglas partition was not only up between myself and the driver, it was up between myself and the rest of the world.

As we smoothly wound our way through the windy canyons of downtown Chicago, I was aware of being very close to the resolution of the investigation. One way or the other. If this was a trap, I was ready. If the driver truly believed I was Derrick Price, then I had successfully, albeit by dumb luck, infiltrated myself into the heart of the operation. I was ready for that, too.

I thought of something Karl Wallenda, the father of the Flying Wallendas, had once said. It was on the day immediately following the worst tragedy that had ever befallen the famous circus high-wire act. Less than twenty-four hours earlier, three members of his family had fallen to their deaths before thousands of horror-stricken onlookers when the seven-man pyramid had collapsed. Reporters had asked Wallenda how he could go back out on the wire so soon after the accident. "Life," replied Wallenda, "is always on the wire."

Yes indeed.

From the direction of what sun there was, we seemed to be heading in a vaguely south and westerly direction. Chicago, of course, has always been a city of neighborhoods, and a great many of them seemed to be flashing by the window of the limo. The faces were now predominantly black and brown and yellow but in one of these neighborhoods about sixty-five years ago, my father had been a little boy. When he was about ten he'd spent the summer working for a Polish man selling vegetables to housewives. The Polish guy rented a horse and cart and loaded it up at the market, then proceeded down the streets and alleyways of the West Side, shouting his wares in at least five languages. My dad rode on top of the cart. It was the first horse he'd ever seen in his life.

Clotheslines stretched like medieval banners across every dark, sooty alley as the horse and cart plodded along, the vegetable peddler screamed his wares, and my father ran the purchases up to the housewives living on the higher floors. To this day, my father remembers his employer shouting one word much more often than any other. The word was *kartofle*. It means "potatoes" in Polish.

Sixty-five years later, my father's son was riding in a sleek limo down the same streets, looking, no doubt, at some of the same old brick buildings now boarded up, clinging to each other for dear life. The vegetable peddler was gone. The horse and cart were gone. The housewives were gone. Their omnipresent clotheslines were gone. All that remained were some trashed-out vacant lots, a few sad old buildings, and an occasional dark, sooty alleyway leading from nowhere to nowhere.

I put the window down for a moment. The back of the limo filled up with an almost primordial cold that seemed to come from somebody else's ice age. I stared out at the desolate landscape where every now and then the dull glint of an old streetcar track became visible just below the surface of the worn-out pavement like the scarred, submerged, hard-to-find veins of a dying junkie.

"Kartofle," I said.

No one was there to hear me except the driver and he just kept his eyes on the road. Either he wasn't Polish or he didn't want any potatoes.

Chapter Twenty-Nine

The limo pulled off to the left across a potholed patch of asphalt that looked like runway number three at Sarajevo International. Taking a meeting of this nature, I reflected, not for the first time on the journey, was like taking your life in your hands. Of course, you had to do something with your hands. It was also a good idea, occasionally, to do something with your head.

The sun was now breaking through the cloud layer, but things did not seem to be measurably warming up. If anything, a cold chill appeared to be moving through the limo, though I'd put the window up some time ago. I thought about asking the driver to adjust the thermostat, but decided to let it slide. Is it cold or is it me is a question that few of us ever truly resolve during the course of our lives. Anyway, he was slowing the limo down now and looking intently toward the side of a nearby warehouse. I didn't want to disrupt his driving patterns this late in the game.

Obviously, the driver thought we were supposed to be meeting someone, but nobody seemed to be around. Just a few rats running along in a ditch, and even they appeared to be only of the four-legged variety. The driver pulled up closer to the warehouse. Then he stopped the car.

"Terribly sorry, Mr. Price," he said, without turning his head. "They should be along any moment now. They probably got held up in traffic." This was a long speech for the driver.

"Very possibly," I said. On this trip, it was a rather long speech for me, too.

The limo driver and I sat in our respective seats and waited. I looked bleakly out the window at the desolate patches of dirt and weeds. If there was going to be a meeting out here it wasn't going to be the kind where the young executive stands up and shows off his multicolored pie charts from Kinko's. But I'd known that long before I'd gotten in the limo. That was why I'd come to Chicago. To make something happen. Everybody's got to die sometime, I figured. Either you die suddenly at the hands of strangers near an abandoned warehouse or you die of ennui sitting around your house wondering how you're going to die. I tell you, it's no way to live.

A dark blue Lincoln Town Car pulled slowly into view from the far corner of the warehouse. It stopped about half a shopping mall away. There were two men sitting in the front seat. Suddenly the city seemed very quiet, distant somehow, though it was everywhere around me. Like the fly that buzzed when Emily Dickinson died.

"One moment, Mr. Price," said the driver, as he opened his door. Then he himself buzzed off in the direction of the newcomers.

I watched. I waited. I worried. There wasn't a hell of a lot else I could do. Since no one had known I was coming to Chicago, except Rambam and McGovern, it seemed unlikely that this meeting, or trap, or scene from *The French Connection,* was being played out for my benefit. Whatever was meant to happen was meant to happen to Derrick Price. Whether or not he existed was something for fans of Kant and Kierkegaard to kick around when they got through discussing whether or not the tree falling in the empty forest makes any noise. The point was, somebody *thought* there was a Derrick Price. If Rambam was right and Price had died seven years ago, how would they ever know he wasn't me?

It was all very confusing, so just for the fun of it I reached for the door handle. My driver, I noticed, was now talking to the guys in the Town Car, and none of them seemed to be too interested in me. If I was going to use my getaway sticks, now was the time. I pulled the door handle. Nothing happened. I pushed every button and turned every switch I could find and pulled the door handle again. No joy for Derrick. The Plexiglas shield was up. The driver had locked me in.

This was not a particularly good sign, but, as events transpired, there wasn't a lot of time to ponder its implications. My driver got into the back of the Town Car and off it sped in the direction it had come. No "Terribly sorry, Mr. Price." Not so much as a wave.

I have often contended that it's a small step from the limo to the gutter. Rarely, however, have I articulated the corollary to that notion. That being, if you never take that small step from the limo to the gutter, something even more tedious inevitably happens.

Tedium on this occasion manifested itself in the form of two men wearing ski masks whom I could now see approaching the limo from the back. They moved methodically up to the limo in the frozen sunlight like two guys coming to work at a carwash. They emptied the contents of two large gasoline cans onto the limo. Then they stood back and one of the ski masks took out a pack of cigarettes and a book of matches. He cupped his hands near his face and lit the cigarette like the Marlboro Man. Then he tossed the match onto the limo.

At least I would be going in style, I remember thinking in the split second before the entire landscape seemed to ignite with a rather singular swooshing sound. Through the flames, I scanned the near horizon just in time to see the two ski masks scurry into the distance, jump into a station wagon, and fishtail it out of there. I fought down a cold, visceral fear as I pounded on the windows and tried and failed repeatedly to open the doors. Not a living soul seemed to be stirring anywhere in the vicinity. Even the rats in the ditches had headed for safer ground.

It did not look as though I was going to find Derrick Price on this trip. Leaning Jesus, as well, would have to wait for another incarnation. Like Nellie Fox, the great second baseman for the Chicago White Sox who should've made it into the Hall of Fame but never did because he died at the wrong time, I was oh-and-two. If I couldn't get out of this limo pretty damn fast, I'd be oh-and-three. Out of there. Grab some bench. Die at the wrong time. Like Nellie Fox. Like Lefty Frizzell. Very important in baseball, as in country music, to die at precisely the right time. Otherwise, you might as well drive your car into a tree in high school. Nobody's ever going to remember you except for a few purists and if there's one thing the world doesn't need it's a few purists. But base-

118

ball and country music are not life. They are more fun, more colorful, and often more meaningful than life, but they're not life. In the game of life almost no one comes out a winner and, even if you're a saint or a martyr, it's always the wrong time to die.

I stared, mesmerized, at the window to my right. As the flames danced across the glass to lick the limo, the dark window tinting was beginning to bubble and melt and drip. A strange pattern seemed to be forming there that did little to assuage my fears. It was Joan of Arc with her hair on fire.

Chapter Thirty

On the first day of classes in the second grade at Edgar Allan Poe Elementary School in Houston, Texas, it became apparent to me and my little classmates that something was terribly wrong. Larry Duckworth, the fat kid with ringworm and the Hopalong Cassidy lunch kit, was not in his front-row seat. From what us kids could piece together later, considering our ignorance at the time of both death and geography, he'd managed to drown on the last day of summer vacation at some place called Lake Stupid along the Texas-Israeli border. The second-grade teacher, Mrs. Necrophiliac, never explained what had happened to the kid. As the whole class stared in wonderment and confusion at the empty chair, all she said to us was that Larry Duckworth had stepped on a rainbow.

Now, almost half a century later and just within sight of the pot of gold, I felt with a dead certainty that I was as perilously close as I was ever going to get to stepping on a rainbow myself. Being trapped inside a burning limo in a desolate area of a strange city will do wonders for speeding up your thought processes. Not that I'd completely solved the case or anything. But shards of information and snippets of conversation were powering through the tiny Tokyo subways of my brain at such a rate as to make me at last realize that I'd been searching for the wrong man.

There'd been a multitude of little red flags all along the parade route, now that I thought about it, and it was just a damn shame that it'd taken a multitude of little red flames for me to finally see the little red flags. Maybe it was something Polly Price had said about McGovern. She'd known he was a journalist, yet she wasn't even from New York. Maybe it was the whole style and scale of the adventures that had befallen Washington Ratso and myself in our nation's capital. Maybe it was what Rambam, the world's greatest hard-boiled computer expert, had turned up on Derrick Price. Maybe it was what he hadn't been able to turn up. Maybe it was the close proximity of McGovern's problems, Polly Price's problems, and my own problems. Everybody had problems, of course, but this was ridiculous. When the driver came back I'd really have to tell him to turn down the damn thermostat. I felt like I was burning up. Maybe it was the almost predatory way that Polly had looked at McGovern that night at Asti's. Maybe it was the fact that if you're sure you're going to kill a guy who's trapped inside a limo and you know he'll never be able to identify you until he sees you in hell, the party is usually ski mask optional.

It all added up to a whole wagonload of maybe's, and now, as near as I could calculate before my own personal computer became hard-boiled, there was only one maybe left. Maybe I could kick out that Plexiglas divider before I was transformed irrevocably into fricassee of Friedman. Plexiglas is not really plastic and not really glass and not really what you'd like to have blocking your last exit to Brooklyn. It has been known to bend slightly, however, and eventually, if the proper force and rhythm are applied, to buckle. It has also been known to melt, but so have cowboy hats and amateur private investigators and I wasn't planning to stick around for that particular chemistry class if I could borrow somebody's notes and make it up later.

You've got to get your kicks in life while you can, and in my corner I had a sturdy pair of brontosaurus foreskin boots and six months of repressed karate classes that I'd taken years ago along with my pal Sal Lorello from the talented black belt Neil Davino in Mount Kisco, New York. Neil was such a great karate expert that he couldn't even join the army. He was afraid if he ever saluted he might kill himself. Neil Davino could've kicked out the partition in a New York second and, judging from the heat inside the limo, there was only a handful of them left. Neil wasn't around, however, and I was, and it was undeniably time to drop-kick me Jesus through the goalposts of life.

My first few efforts were rather disappointing but as the crackling and hissing noises grew louder and the interior of the limo began to resemble the smoking car on the City of New Orleans, I started to get the hang of it. It might've been my imagination but the partition seemed to be giving a little more each time I kicked. I was no longer sure what was happening. Possibly the sea was playing tricks on me. But I continued to attack the divider with a series of measured, if somewhat frantic, kicks, all of them focusing on follow-through. By the time the damn thing buckled I felt like a Rockette on angel dust, but I knew Neil Davino would've been proud.

It didn't take Huey Long to build a bridge in Louisiana and it didn't take me long to collect my belongings and leapfrog over the seat and out the unlocked front door of the limo. In no time at all I was out on the windswept, frozen corner of Nightmare Alley and Desolation Row looking for a working pay phone to call my cousin Rachel Samet. It was a close call, but I made it. Then all I had to do was wait around and try to blend into the rotten woodwork and terrifying twilight of cosmic confusion and posttraumatic stress from my near-death out-of-limo experience.

By the time Rachel's car pulled up to the curb I was a half-frozen, spinning ghost, halfheartedly hoping that somewhere amongst the ruins of the city I'd run into Leaning Jesus. Hell, I thought, *any* Jesus would do.

Rachel leaned across the front seat and held the door open for me. I got in, slightly feverish and still shaking from the cold and the heat, and gave her a quick hug. Then she pulled away from the curb and we headed out to her apartment.

"So what brings you to Chicago?" she said.

Chapter Thirty-One

Rachel Samet's apartment was north of the city and provided the perfect sanctuary for me to soothe the singed feathers on my cowboy hat, make a few phone calls to New York, and try to decide how to answer the question "So what brings you to Chicago?" It wasn't really a hard question, but the answer, rather maddeningly, seemed to be in a state of continuous evolution. A strange sense of foreboding and a somewhat persistent, prickly sensation along the back of my neck kept convincing me that I'd come to the right place for the wrong reason.

Rachel was twenty-six years old, very bright, very pretty, and an interior designer by trade, who'd made her apartment just beautifully appointed enough to make a guy like me feel slightly uncomfortable. Rachel's father, Dr. Eli T. Samet, a brilliant surgeon, had been my mother's younger brother until both of them had stepped on a rainbow. Eli had been the "doctor in Chicago" that I'd made reference to in the song "Rapid City, South Dakota," which, to my knowledge, was the first pro-choice country song. It is also, to my knowledge, the only pro-choice country song.

"Here's a little bit of spiritual trivia for you," I said, trying to make the best out of my scattered thoughts and sordid appearance. "What is the only bird in the world that has two feathers for every quill?" I took off my cowboy hat and showed Rachel the two feathers. They were only very slightly singed.

"I'm stumped," said Rachel, who obviously didn't give a damn but was trying her best to be an accommodating hostess to her elder cousin, who was shaping up to be a rather troubled, tormented house pest. She walked over to the cabinet and came back with a large unopened bottle of Wild Turkey, which she placed on the table before me.

"There's another bird I like," I said, as Rachel brought some glasses and sat down across from me at the table.

Sometimes, when you're in a confused state of mind, it's hard to talk to a friend or a relative that you haven't seen in a while. But as the snake piss started flowing, so did the conversation and soon we'd covered Rachel's two cats and my cat, whom Stephanie DuPont had agreed orally to take care of in my unexpected absence. Stephanie had not been ecstatic about the arrangement, but somehow I trusted her, which was more than I could currently say about clients or limo drivers, or just about anyone else in the world.

Except possibly Cousin Rachel. I don't know if it was just the Wild Turkey gobbling or whether I badly needed to talk the situation over with a fairly objective friendly human being, but in the next two and a half hours I rolled out the whole megillah for Rachel, her two cats, and a life-size wooden Indian that stood stolidly in Rachel's apartment and vaguely resembled Kawliga's smarter older brother. I also wanted to hear myself tell the story again just to see if I'd been as careless, blundering, and unobservant as I thought I'd been. Apparently, I had.

At one point in my dissertation I got up to make three phone calls and then to visit the little detective's room, where evidence of Rachel's designer talents made me mildly uncomfortable urinating. Give me a brick wall in an alley, I thought. Give me a field in Texas under a starry sky. Give me a chance to sort this craziness out in my brain.

Rambam's computer had kept burping every time the name Derrick Price came up. He'd never seen anything like it, he'd said. He'd also commented that anyone who really wanted to burn a vehicle burned it from the bottom up instead of the top down. "Either they weren't trying to kill you or they fucked up," he added. I told him either one was fine with me. McGovern's line was busy. So was Polly Price's. I flushed the dumper and went back to finish my story without washing my hands as all employees must. It was one of the small advantages to being your own boss. Also, I didn't want to soil Cousin Rachel's beautifully mounted hand towels. At any rate, I doubted seriously if a germ from my penis would jump onto my hand and wind up killing me. It hadn't happened yet and there'd been lots of opportunities. Or, if it had happened, I didn't know about it. The disease had been very slow in developing. Even slower than I'd been in figuring out what had brought me to Chicago.

"So that's the whole turbulent, sometimes rather tedious affair," I said, a short while later as I noticed the bottle was nearing the midway mark. "As a polite, but disinterested observer, I've told you everything from the original phone call from Polly Price to the call I made to you earlier this evening when I popped out of the burning limo like a gourmet scion of Orville Redenbacher. What do you make of it, Rachel?"

"Well, Kinky, I've never been involved in anything like this before, searching for somebody's husband. All the weird things that've happened to your friend McGovern. The close scrapes you got into in Washington and now here in Chicago. You've had a lot more experience than I have at—"

"C'mon, Rachel, don't massage my wilted ego at a time like this. Get to the chorus, Boris. What do you really think is happening?"

"Sounds like someone's sending you on a wild goose chase," said Rachel.

"There's a bird I *don't* like," I said.

Chapter Thirty-Two

Rachel steered me steadily to the spare bedroom so I could take a short power nap, but I didn't sleep. I kept empathizing rather heavily with a fictional character named Jabez Wilson. Jabez Wilson had red hair and I didn't, but otherwise it seemed that the two of us had a hell of a lot in common. For those Americans who may feel fairly foggy in their Sherlock Holmes area, Jabez Wilson was the owner of a pawnshop who came to the great detective with a strange story. Wilson's shop assistant, a man named Vincent Spaulding, who'd taken the job at half wages, had approached his boss several months before with a hot news item. Ezekiah Hopkins, an extremely eccentric American millionaire, had recently croaked, leaving his loved ones, after they'd carefully perused his will, in somewhat of a snit.

Apparently, Hopkins, being a redhead himself, and very possibly having very little inside his head, had left his vast fortune in the hands of trustees along with a set of somewhat peculiar—especially to the minds of the greedy, rather repellent relatives—instructions. The money was to be reserved expressly to provide easy berths for men all over the world who had hair of a color similar to Ezekiah Hopkins. Thus was born one of Sherlock's most convoluted and baffling cases, that of "The Red-Headed League."

Jabez Wilson had dutifully gone to a certain

address where he was informed that if he remained at that address each working day copying the *Encyclopaedia Britannica,* he would indeed find it to be a financial pleasure. He had and it was. Unfortunately for Mr. Wilson, however, Ezekiah Hopkins's largess did not continue for terribly long. About two months after beginning the monumental and somewhat ludicrous task, he came to work one morning to find a rather unsettling notice tacked to the door. It read:

The Red-Headed League
Is
Dissolved
October 9, 1890

Jabez Wilson was, to say the least, extremely irritated. He'd only gotten as far as "asshole." That was about as far as I'd gotten, too. I just wasn't quite certain who the asshole was.

As I lay in Rachel Samet's spare bed with a strange cat, it became glaringly apparent to me that my actions and efforts of the past few weeks had been equally as meaningless as those of Jabez Wilson in copying the *Encyclopaedia Britannica.* If anything, Wilson had probably learned more. But what seemed truly disturbing to me was my growing belief that both Jabez Wilson and I had been sucked, fucked, and cajoled into our various fruitless endeavors for precisely the same reason. Somebody had clearly wanted both of us out of the way.

In Jabez Wilson's case, The Red-Headed League itself had merely been a clever device to lure him away from his own office so he wouldn't lamp on to the fact that tunneling was occurring directly beneath him to the bank vault next door. For

127

Sherlock Holmes, the whole affair had hardly amounted to a three-pipe problem. In the pale light of the twentieth century, however, life is quite another story. Our lives today come very close to being defined by something Edgar Allen Poe, even before Sherlock, had once observed about the game of chess: "Complex without being profound."

Sherlock, of course, was not here to help me. He was sitting on my desk in New York, surrounding a precious handful of Habana Montecristo #2 cigars Ratso had belatedly sent over, and doing his best to keep the dust and cat hair out of his timeless, all-knowing, penetrating porcelain eyes. It fell entirely to me to figure out what it was that had piqued someone's interest about my somewhat bohemian, often rather melancholy, existence to such a degree that they'd find it important to try to lure me away from New York. In my life and my loft, both figuratively and literally speaking, and much to my own private disappointment, there did not appear to be any bank vault. My life lately, at least before Polly Price had strolled into it, could be fully captured in one word. It was the same word that Captain John Smith had used to describe his forty years at sea in his last interview before sailing off at the helm of the *Titanic*. The word was "uneventful."

Yet I suspected that Cousin Rachel was right. Chicago had been a wild goose chase. Now that I thought about it, so had Washington. There I'd been winged. Here I'd been slightly defrosted in an extremely expensive microwave on wheels. In both instances, money was clearly no object for these people. Torching a new limousine or leaving around a busted valise full of Irving Berlin's

White Christmas meant nothing to these folks. Nor—and this was significant—did they particularly seem to want to croak me. Lord knows they had had plenty of opportunities. "Either they weren't trying to kill you or they fucked up," Rambam had told me on the phone. After that, he'd launched into a rather laborious technical treatise on how to make your own napalm by dissolving Styrofoam cups in gasoline and then laying out this little jellied dessert underneath an unsuspecting vehicle. I'd nodded off about half-way through Rambam's tutorial, but I'd effectively grasped the subject matter. They wanted to frighten me maybe. They wanted to send me on my merry way looking for the next clue in some mindless scavenger hunt. But they weren't trying to croak me. If they'd wanted to croak me, they would've already croaked me. These kinds of people did not fuck up.

Now I thought back to the break-in at my loft that had occurred when I was out playing with Ratso in my nation's capital. Maybe they'd only lifted Derrick's papers to cover for what they were really after. The bank vault had to be somewhere in my loft or in my life. Had to be. These guys operated like pros. One could only assume they knew what they were searching for. If that was indeed true, the bastards were ten steps ahead of the rest of us.

If I was going to follow Sherlockian dictum, my task was to offload that which was impossible, and whatever was left, no matter how improbable, had to be the truth. It was improbable, all right. I'd most likely suspected it for some little time, but it was only now, as I lay in Cousin Rachel's guest room counting flowers on the wall that I admitted finally to myself what that improbable thing was that had to be the truth. Had to be what these mysterious people were really after.

It was not me they wanted. It wasn't even Derrick Price. It was McGovern.

It was a wildly improbable idea, but it explained a lot of things. Why I couldn't find Derrick Price. Why McGovern was being followed, spied upon, and harassed. Why they wanted me out of the way so they could get to him more easily. Maybe it all had to do with Leaning Jesus and whatever he'd once given to McGovern that he now evidently wanted back. Of course, Leaning Jesus was almost certainly dead, but that made things only a little more improbable than they already were.

I got out of the little bed and walked over to the antique-style designer telephone. I dialed McGovern's number. It was still busy. I hesitated for just a moment and then I called Polly Price's number. Her number was also still busy.

I walked out onto the little patio and looked across at the North Shore. I lit a cigar and watched as people painted lights onto the dark velvet of the city night. It was time for me to get busy, too.

Chapter Thirty-Three

It was crowding Cinderella time when Cousin Rachel and I pulled over to the side of the street to look at the map again. It wasn't the kind of neighborhood you'd really want to be in at Cinderella time or at any other time for that matter. But it hadn't always been this way. There was a time, back in the forties and fifties, when guys like Redd Foxx played Negro clubs in this neighborhood. It was a very happenin' place in those days. According to the notes I'd made from my earlier conversations with McGovern, one of the hottest venues here on the South Shore had once been a place called the Ambassador Club. The old Ambo, as it was called, had been located at the corner of 79th and Kingston. It had been owned by a man named Leaning Jesus.

"Rachel, I've got a bad feeling about dragging you into all this. I'm not certain exactly what it is but I do know it could be hazardous to your health."

"Don't be silly. Give me the map."

"I'm not kidding. Someone's been tailing me around New York. Then they show up in Washington. Now they're here in Chicago."

"You sure you're not just getting paranoid?"

"The only thing I'm sure of is that I left my fucking reading glasses in the limo."

"So give me the map."

I gave her the map. She studied it for a moment with the small flashlight that we'd picked up at the last convenience store before we'd left civilization as we knew it. It didn't take long for her to pinpoint our current location and the location of 79th and Kingston. It was only a bad dream away.

I looked into the rearview mirror again but saw no sign of any vehicle in the vicinity. All I saw was a ragged old man with a bottle in his hand vomiting in the gutter. Could've been Edgar Allan Poe or Ira Hayes or Stephen Foster. Could've been me, I thought, given the wrong bloodlines and the right heartbreak.

"Listen, Rachel, I just have a feeling your mother wouldn't want you to be involved in this."

"Mom doesn't have to know," she said, sounding suddenly very young.

"That's true."

"Besides, something tells me that my dad approves."

I suspected she was right. If things went wrong, of course, I might be catching hell a little sooner than I'd planned.

"Drive on," I said.

As we closed in on the area of Leaning Jesus's old haunts, the street seemed to become a little more populated, if you wanted to call it that. The people seemed to cling to the shadows and the shadows seemed to cling to the people. Like heathens or whores or other biblical types, they huddled together beneath burned-out streetlights waiting for the sun to take them away.

"Kind of gives you the creeps," said Rachel.

"That's correct," I said, "and just to get your mind off it, this might be the time to tell you that the only bird with two feathers for each quill is the emu."

"I thought the emu was extinct."

"Not yet, but we're working on it."

By the time we got to the corner where the old Ambo Club had been, the people and the shadows had gone away and so had just about everything else. The corner was as quiet as a country graveyard with nothing and no one stirring anywhere, and that was fine with me. The old building on the corner might've once been a jumpin' joint but now stood somber as a shipwreck on the forgotten floor of some uncharted sea Columbus missed on his way to discovering the Bank of America.

Rachel parked the car across the street from what had once been the Ambo. At least I hoped it had once been the Ambo. Everything else in the area looked about as promising as a lunar landscape. I told Rachel I was only going to pop inside the place for a moment and she was to wait inside the car with doors locked and lights off.

"Can I play the radio, daddy?"

"NO. And if you see anyone at all come near the car I want you to make this place sound like rush hour in the Loop."

"Don't worry," said Rachel. "I'll honk if I love Leaning Jesus."

I took my little flashlight and headed for the door of the dark, godforsaken old structure. It didn't look like a major B & E job because the front door was standing open off its hinges. Forty, fifty, maybe sixty years ago this place might've been brimming with guys and dolls and machine guns and money and laughter and liquor and excitement and intrigue. You might've even had to say "Joe sent me" to get in. I wasn't sure who had sent me, but whoever it was had a pretty sick sense of humor. It was a stretch to imagine that there could be any relic of the past in this old house that could help explain the events occurring in McGovern's life or my life today. It was a long shot but it was the only shot I had. I knew what I was looking for. I had to give Leaning Jesus a name.

I quickly moved through the front of the house, shining the flashlight around enough to show me that it'd been totally trashed through decades of disuse. It looked like a crack house that had seen better days. On the floor, in the place of furniture, were old boxes, blankets, broken wine bottles, used butane lighters, pads of dirty steel wool to smoke crack through, and an old shopping cart that stood in a cobwebbed corner. It was asleep. Waiting for its happy suburban shopper to come.

I wasn't sure yet if indeed this had ever been the old Ambo Club that McGovern had talked about so glowingly. If it truly was the place, generations of life's refugees had come here since Leaning Jesus had lurched off the screen. From the look of the place, I doubted if Joe had sent any of them. Maybe another Jesus had.

I didn't want to leave Rachel in the car too long and I didn't want to stay in this hellhole of a house too long so I worked my way toward the back of the place, where McGovern had said the bar and kitchen used to be. I found what must've been the cooking area, but there was no one in the kitchen with Dinah strummin' on the ol' banjo. I had to duck around and under old rusted pipes everywhere, some of them still dripping onto places where the floor was rotting away. It was like watching ancient gnarled limbs leaking the lifeblood of a bygone era.

On a dusty shelf nearby was a rain-soaked makeup and cosmetics kit, possibly left by street prostitutes who'd come here to get high between tricks. Then I shined the light in the far corner and saw the old beauty herself. She'd probably been too heavy for looters to take away like almost everything else that had once been in the place. I could almost smell the old Italian pasta sauces cooking. I could almost see Leaning Jesus himself coming by at regular intervals to stir the pots with a wooden spoon as they simmered away forever. Well, almost forever. It was a huge, old-fashioned gas stove with iron feet like you used to find on some old bathtubs.

My gaze wandered to the black, greasy wall just

behind the big gas stove. That was where I found them. The food and liquor licenses for the Ambassador Club. They looked like a museum display of the Magna Carta, faded like the years themselves, but still legible enough to reveal a name. Here was something very few people, including McGovern, had known.

Leaning Jesus's name was Jim Pollard.

There was even a legible home address on one of the tattered yellow documents. Leaning Jesus was almost certainly dead, according to my calculations, but surely there must be friends or family still loitering around where he'd once lived. And it wasn't easy to forget a guy named Leaning Jesus. Suddenly, I was very excited. I felt almost sure Polly Price had set up wild goose chases for me in Washington and Chicago so that she could get at McGovern. She'd hired me to pursue her imaginary husband because she knew McGovern was confiding in me about Leaning Jesus. Did that make sense? No. But it got worse. She'd hired me before I'd even told her about McGovern or Leaning Jesus. What did that suggest? And Leaning Jesus had been Al Capone's chef. *Bon appetit* and curiouser and curiouser.

I was scribbling Pollard's name and his home address in my little private investigator's notebook when I heard a voice in the darkness behind me.

"What up?" it said.

Then I heard another voice from somewhere a little closer.

"Hey, white boy," it said. "Got any money?"

All the flashlight was doing was revealing my location, so I killed it and tried to move away into the semidarkness. I could see the afterimages of two large, dark forms lumbering toward me. From the way they moved and sounded they were obviously sprung on crack. I slid quickly into the side room where the prostitutes had maintained their little vanity. I grabbed a half-full can of Aqua Net hairspray, took out my Bic lighter, and waited. I wasn't going to fire until I saw the whites of their eyes.

They came at me a little faster than I'd expected. I got off one strong shot of aerosol over the tiny lit flame of the Bic, which roared through the little room like a fire out of hell. But crack addicts are used to fire. I was stumbling around in the darkness, hoping that the exits were well lit, when a large figure loomed up in front of me and hit me over the head with what appeared to be a table leg.

The last thing I remember hearing before I became totally out where the buses don't run was a car honking somewhere out in the street.

Chapter Thirty-Four

I woke up in a strange room with a strange woman. It wasn't the first time, but it felt like the worst time. My orbs were having some difficulty focusing, and it sounded like some chubby little kid was inside my head warming up for his bassoon recital. Then my eyes and ears began to clear and I realized I was flat on my back in the Ambo Club with celestial light shining on my face as I listened to the voice of an angel. The angel had a slight Chicago accent.

"They took your wallet and your watch," she said, "but they left your cowboy hat and this little notebook you were scribbling in."

"Rachel?"

"I thought I saw a fire inside, so I started honking my horn, and a few moments later two men started running south down the street."

"We'll head north."

"How many fingers am I holding up?"

"Very funny, Rachel."

"Well, it's what you deserve for coming in here alone and almost getting yourself killed. If it hadn't been for you wearing this cowboy hat and me honking the horn—"

"Maybe God protects middle-aged Jewish amateur detectives," I said, sitting up painfully and putting the cowboy hat gently back on my head.

"And children, drunks, and fools," said Rachel disapprovingly.

"Yep," I said, looking at my little notebook, "He keeps Himself pretty busy, but so do we. And we ain't through yet tonight."

"What?" said Rachel. "You've got to be crazy."

"As Willie Nelson once told me: 'If you ain't crazy, there's something wrong with you.'"

I got up a little less gracefully than I would've liked and showed Rachel the address where I believed Leaning Jesus had once lived. She took the notebook a bit reluctantly but, after a brief hesitation, shined the flashlight on the page.

"I remember McGovern saying that Leaning Jesus used to walk home from here after the bar closed, so it couldn't be too far. He used to carry a sawed-off shotgun inside a brown paper bag and everybody knew it, so nobody fucked with him. Pardon my Shakespeare."

"You *are* getting middle-aged."

"Anyway, he gave a whole new definition to brown-baggin' it. Let's check out this address on the map and go for a little late-night ride, baby."

"Right away, General Custer."

A few moments later we were safely inside the car, studying the map together. One headache more or less didn't bother me much if I was as close as I thought I was to untangling the enigma that was Leaning Jesus. A lot of ideas were beginning to flow in and out of my mind, no doubt shaken loose by the contact between my head and the table leg. Sort of like the time Isaac Newton was sitting under a tree and got hit on the head by the gravity-driven apple. Some of the ideas were quite preposterous, even to my own current mildly amphibious thought processes. But some of them were starting to make an eerie kind of sense to me. I thought I'd try one of them out on Rachel as she drove the little car warily through the silent, desolate streets.

"Think about this, Cousin Rachel. Al Capone went away sometime in the thirties—"

"Went away?"

"To prison. Tax evasion. Don't interrupt your elders."

"You got that right."

"I'm a little rusty on the time lines, but I remember he was stabbed but only wounded at Alcatraz by a Texas bank robber named James Lucas who was no relation to Old Ben Lucas who had a lot of mucous—"

"That's disgusting."

"That's what Al thought. So anyway, McGovern left Chicago in sixty-eight to go to New York. The only possible connection between Al Capone and Mike McGovern was Leaning Jesus. Now what does that suggest to you?"

"That Al Pacino may play McGovern in *God-*

father, Part Five?"

"No, dear—"

Suddenly Rachel swerved the car to the curb with an enthusiasm that almost sent my head spinning again.

"That's it," she said excitedly. "That's the address. It's two o'clock in the morning and all the lights are on. Do you think Leaning Jesus could still be living there?"

"It's either him or Tom Bodet," I said.

Chapter Thirty-Five

On the South Side of Chicago, as in almost every other urban center of America today, even a Jehovah's Witness knows it's not particularly best foot forward to knock on someone's door at two o'clock in the morning. Nevertheless, it was mildly frustrating to have gotten parboiled in the backseat of a limousine and then bopped on the head by some australopithecine, all so I could sit out at the curb and gaze at a house that was lit up like a Christmas tree in Las Vegas. If someone inside had some answers I wanted them now. The more I thought about it, the more concerned I was becoming about the uneasy state of McGovern's health, education, and welfare.

As somewhat of a past expert on various forms of substance abuse myself, I knew that different drugs produce different perceptions of what for most normal, nonusing, good little church workers remains the same hideously boring, stultifyingly dull workaday treadmill of an existence. Not only will those who freely partake of drugs and alcohol see reality differently, but their perceptions may vary greatly from one individual to another depending upon precisely how they mix their John Belushi cocktails. For instance, it is not at all uncommon for the speed freak to look repeatedly out between his venetian blinds in the middle of the night and think he sees the deputy sheriff lurking in the backyard. No one on cocaine has ever looked through the venetian blinds and seen a deputy sheriff. For the children of the snow it has to be the CIA, Interpol, or maybe a crack Gurkha unit, and I do mean crack. And when you pour alcohol on top of all this, things can really start to get a little wiggy.

But what was bothering me went far deeper than the blurred edges of reality and the perceptions of man or the lack of these perceptions. McGovern was a veteran of the fifth estate. As a seasoned journalist who'd traveled the world and plumbed the minds of men to record what he'd observed, he wasn't all that likely to be this far off the tracks. What if all the things McGovern thought were happening to him were really happening to him? If that were indeed the case, McGovern might currently be in some rather deep, dangerous waters. Far deeper than the denizens of California hot tubs ever dream of.

"We're going in," I said.

"I don't know, admiral," said Rachel, "but don't you think we should wait till the first light of dawn?"

"By the first light of dawn," I said, "I plan to be drinking a Bloody Mary on an aircraft headed for New York."

"That's better than flying back to Texas in a pine box."

"I'll mention it to my travel agent," I said, as I

got out of the car. "You can come with me if you like."

"I think I'd better," said Rachel.

The path to Leaning Jesus's old residence was well kept and well lit, with the door and the windows of the place being protected, of course, by heavy bars. It almost made me a little homesick for New York.

I didn't have a prepared Rotary luncheon speech in my mind. I just hoped, as we stepped up onto the little front porch, that the name Leaning Jesus would mean something here. If it didn't, I could always try pissing up a rope for an encore.

I knocked on the door.

After a moment or two, steps could be heard inside the house. Then a shadow moved across the windowshade in the direction of the front door.

"Who is it?" came a wary voice from the other side of the door.

"Friends of Leaning Jesus," I said. Sometimes you have to stretch the truth a little to find out what it is.

We waited.

Soon we were rewarded by the sounds of bolts being unlocked and a chain being removed. Then the door opened to reveal the figure of a man. He appeared to be a gentle soul with gray hair and a smooth, youthful-looking face. I guessed he was about my age.

I introduced myself and Rachel and gave him the briefest of bumper stickers about my search for Leaning Jesus and how I found this address at the old Ambo Club.

"I'm James Pollard Jr.," he said. "Leaning Jesus's son."

Chapter Thirty-Six

"My father died in nineteen sixty-two," he said, as the three of us sat around the kitchen table like the old friends in "Bob Dylan's Dream." "He was hit by the last working streetcar in Chicago. It was sort of a tourist attraction. A real dinosaur. But then again, in many ways, so was my dad."

"Thirty-four years is a long time," I said.

"So they tell me," said Pollard.

As I watched him diligently measuring out coffee for the three of us, I thought that James Pollard Jr. was a lonely man. I wondered briefly whether he was gay or not and decided that it didn't matter to a tree. He had a cute little black dog named Perky, who was currently sitting in Rachel's lap. He had apparently been up at two o'clock in the morning reading. Right now he seemed to be reading my thoughts.

"Perky and I don't often get visitors at this hour of the morning," he said. "In fact, we don't often get visitors much at all these days. It gets a little lonely sometimes, but it's fine with us. Makes up for all the years when my father was alive and the feds wouldn't leave us alone. One of the reasons I let you in tonight is that you look like one of the colorful characters my father would've liked."

I took that as a compliment and found myself starting to like this guy. In many ways, of course, he wasn't so very different from myself.

"If you don't mind," I said, "tell us a little about the feds. Why wouldn't they leave your father alone?"

"How much do you really know about my father?"

"Very little really except that he owned the

Ambassador Club, he was Al Capone's chef, and they called him Leaning Jesus."

"He was much more than Al Capone's chef," said Pollard as he brought the coffee to the table on a little tray. "Capone, at the height of his reign, was such a powerful man that he trusted almost no one. He was like the king of the gypsies. He had a huge extended family, some of whom were even related to him. He was like Napoleon. He had a vast army of soldiers awaiting his every command. Yet he never was able to be very close to these people. He never trusted them. He trusted my father."

Pollard was giving his account with almost no pride or approbation. He spoke dispassionately, as if he were a kindly professor giving a lecture on Pharaoh Esophagus's reign in Ancient Egypt now all but forgotten within the dusty book jackets of what we call history. Of course, yesterday's triumphs and tragedies may well be today's trivia. But as my own father often reminds me, there is no trivia.

"In nineteen thirty-one, just before Capone was convicted on income-tax charges, he summoned his tailor to measure him for several lightweight suits to wear in Miami. Leaning Jesus was there, along with Frankie Rio, one of his many cohorts. 'You don't need to be ordering fancy duds,' said Rio. 'Why don't you have a suit made with stripes on it? You're going to prison.' Then Capone winked at Leaning Jesus. 'The hell I am,' he said. 'I'm going to Florida for a nice long rest and I need some new clothes before I go.'

"Capone never really believed it was over. Leaning Jesus never believed it either. But it was. By that time the gang wars had taken over seven hundred lives, including the notorious St. Valentine's Day Massacre in nineteen twenty-nine when seven survivors of the O'Bannion Gang were lined up and mowed down with machine guns in a North Side garage. I'm sorry. Do you take sugar?"

Rachel and I shook our heads. For whatever reason, possibly his insular lifestyle, Pollard seemed to be opening up to us in almost a cathartic fashion. I didn't want to stop him if he was on a roll. Soon he continued.

"When Capone walked into the big house in Atlanta in May of thirty-two, for all practical purposes he was washed up as a mob boss. Two years later, he was transferred to Alcatraz. Four years after that, the authorities there announced he was a mental patient. He died in nineteen forty-seven in Miami at his Palm Island estate. Doctors said he had the mentality then of a child of twelve. But my father had been in touch with him over the years and also just prior to his death. He said the doctors were crazy, Capone was as sharp as ever."

At this point Perky jumped off Rachel's lap and Pollard seemed precariously close to jumping off the tracks himself for a moment.

"Wait a minute," he said, "this isn't for publication or anything? You're not writing a book, are you?"

"Of course not. I'm just interested in why someone is invoking Leaning Jesus's name to harass and intimidate a friend of mine and why his problems seem to be spilling over on me."

"Leaning Jesus never killed anyone, you understand. That wasn't why the feds hounded him. They knew he was more than a chef. They knew he was Capone's confidant. And they suspected Capone might have transferred a certain vital missing document of his to my father. But the feds never would say exactly what it was and if it existed at all, Leaning Jesus took its nature and its whereabouts with him when he died. After Capone went away and especially after his death, they interrogated my father unmercifully. Tape-recorded interviews with him for hours at a time. Searched this house on many occasions. But by the fifties it had all stopped. Then there was one last gasp in nineteen sixty-two after he died. They went through this place from top to bottom, but they found nothing. They asked me a lot of questions, but there was little I could tell them. Dad never talked to me about his business. Just as well, I suppose."

Tape-recorded interviews, I thought. Getting warmer.

Pollard got up and poured us all a fresh cup of coffee. I asked if I could smoke a cigar. He said he'd like that. It'd remind him of the old times. He went to get an ashtray and I shrugged at Rachel. The guy might not have all the answers but at least he was an accommodating host. God knows, there was a shortage of those these days.

"So when Leaning Jesus died in nineteen sixty-two," I said, as he came back with the ashtray, "that was the last you saw of the feds."

"Until about two months ago," he said.

I stopped my cigar in mid-flight to my mouth. A big piece had just fallen into place here and I knew it. I also knew, somewhat to my discomfort, that we were dealing with a very big puzzle. One that had just spanned eight decades in the time it had taken to drink two cups of coffee.

"This is getting too close for country dancin'," I said. "What was their excuse this time?"

"Somebody'd finally retired at headquarters. They said they were closing the file."

"Did you get the names of any of the agents involved?"

"I'm afraid not. Of course, they didn't get anything either. I don't really believe there's anything to get."

I leaned over and patted Perky for a while. The dog looked smarter than many people I knew. I wasn't feeling too bright myself at that moment. Like a character in a long-ago children's story I half remembered, I was leaving Chicago an older but not a particularly wiser bear. The smart thing to do, I thought, would be to hibernate until spring. Bears slept for months at a time in their caves, why couldn't I? Of course, bears didn't have to get up to urinate or feed the cat. And they probably didn't have nightmares unless they were scared of mice. No, that was elephants. Bears probably had nightmares about men. Between mice and men, we could no doubt scare the shit out of anybody. I didn't plan to be having any nightmares, however. As Warren Zevon once recommended: "I'll sleep when I'm dead." And that, if I wasn't very careful, could well be sooner instead of later.

I was still patting Perky and now, half consciously, I suppose, I began singing to him. It was a little thing I'd picked up from the old Big John and Sparky radio show, a program I listened to often as a child. Quite possibly, if what the doctors said was true about Capone, he and I might've been listening at the same time.

"'If you go down to the woods today
you're in for a big surprise
If you go down to the woods today

146

you'd better go in disguise. . . .'"

Perky seemed to be listening to the song rather intently. James Pollard Jr. appeared to be staring at me rather intently.

"'Dah dah dah dah dah dah dah dah dah
Dah dah dah dah dah dah dah dah
Today's the day the teddy bears have
their Pic—nic. . . .'"

"Well," said Rachel, "I think it's about time for us to be going."

"I just have one more question," I said. "Suppose for just a moment that this mysterious document did exist and that Capone did actually entrust it to Leaning Jesus before he went away. Now, cast your mind back, Mr. Pollard. Did your father ever allude to anything like that, possibly in a seemingly rather cryptic fashion?"

Pollard thought about it for a moment. Rachel began readying her purse for departure. Perky wagged her tail beside my chair, more than likely hoping for another verse of the Big John and Sparky theme song.

"Not that I remember," said Pollard, with a bit of hesitation. But there was something in his manner that was keeping me in the game.

"Was there anything he ever said, that comes back to you now, that you didn't understand? Anything peculiar that didn't make sense?"

Rachel and I were standing now. So was Perky. Pollard was standing by his coffee cup, leaning against the counter, possibly debating whether or not to spill it.

"Actually," said Pollard, "there was something

147

my father said after the streetcar accident that I didn't understand. It was later that night in the hospital just before he died. Of course, it's possible that his mind had been affected by the accident, because I'm his only son and I know he had a girlfriend for a while, but I would've certainly known if he'd had an illegitimate child."

The kitchen had become very still. In fact, the whole world seemed to have become very still. Pollard, appearing to be half in a trance, looked like he might be prepared to stand there like that forever. After another moment or two I gave him some gentle encouragement.

"Try to recall," I said, "the exact words Leaning Jesus said to you."

Pollard's eyes looked into that hospital room. Perky tried to follow his master's gaze, but, like the feds over the years, he came up short.

"The last words my father spoke made no sense to me whatsoever. He looked up at me from the hospital bed and grabbed my arm tightly. All he said was: 'The kid. Where's the kid?'"

Chapter Thirty-Seven

My flight back to New York was, to quote Captain John Smith of the *Titanic* again, "uneventful." Unlike James Pollard Jr., I felt pretty sure I knew who the kid was. I kept asking myself, however, the same question Leaning Jesus had asked on his deathbed: *Where* is the kid? I'd called McGovern's number from O'Hare earlier in the morning, and then again when I landed at La Guardia. The phone rang and rang and rang. No busy signal any longer. No answering machine. No kid.

Not only did I call McGovern's number, but, for good measure, I called Polly Price's number from both airports as well. The results of these efforts were, not terribly surprisingly, the same. Not only was there no kid, there was also no client. It was shaping up to be one honey of a case.

In the cab, on the way over to Vandam, I thought once again of Rambam's rather chauvinistic advice: Never trust a female client. That credo was certainly out of sync with the prevailing attitudes of the times—*The New York Times* or any times, but that didn't necessarily mean it was without merit. A little chauvinism today, quite possibly, might prevent a little tedium tomorrow. But not only was I feeling very distrustful of female clients at the moment, I also was developing a rather low regard for large Irish journalists. In fact, my attitude was strikingly similar to that of Al Capone's toward the end of his life when, like a bloodthirsty, psychotic, paranoid, stubborn, diabolical twelve-year-old, he refused to trust anyone. That attitude may never win you a lot of friends, but it's not a bad one to have if you know you're coming to New York.

"I don't believe it," Rambam was saying later that afternoon as both of us were busy pacing the loft at different diagonals. "The last time I spoke to you, when you were in Chicago, you had *two* clients. Now they're *both* missing."

"Well," I said, "it's easy for something like that to happen. I've been quite busy, you see, copying the *Encyclopaedia Britannica* for the Red-Headed League."

"Did you get as far as the word 'fuckup'?" said Rambam.

"No," I said, "I was waiting for you to help me."

149

"Well, here I am. Of course, you've already broken the first two rules of the private investigator: Never trust a woman client, and never take on a nonpaying client."

"I guess it's just that Christ-like streak in me that keeps coming out."

"If it comes out again," said Rambam, "don't be surprised if somebody takes three little nails and puts you up for the night."

Rambam was very frustrated. I was rather highly agitato myself. And none of this was going down very well with the cat. Cats do not enjoy hearing acrimonious conversations and seldom if ever take part in them. In this case, the cat was hunkering down rather pathetically beside the gurgling espresso machine, partially because the loft was cold, but also, I felt, because she was disappointed by the general absence of human warmth in the place.

"Now look what you've done," I said to Rambam. "You've upset the cat."

"Fuck the cat," said Rambam.

He advanced upon the cat and myself rather angrily, stopping only to pick up a small piece of perfume-scented, pink pastel stationery on the counter. I tried, unsuccessfully, to grab it away from him.

"What do we have here?" said Rambam tauntingly.

"It's nothing," I said. "Just a little love note from Stephanie DuPont. She's back in town and she was taking care of the cat for me while I was in Chicago. Give it to me."

Rambam sniffed the stationery.

"Very nice," he said. Then he shot his cuffs back in an exaggerated preparation to read the letter.

The gesture bore an uncanny resemblance to that of Ed Norton in *The Honeymooners.*

"Let's see what she says," said Rambam, easily frustrating any efforts I made to snatch the paper from him. He cleared his throat several times. Then, much to my chagrin, he read the note out loud.

> You need more cat food, turbo dick. And while you're out shopping, get a life.
>
> Stephanie

"I like a girl who's not afraid to express herself," said Rambam, with a sarcastic smirk.

"She's got a rather caustic sense of humor," I said.

The cat merely closed her eyes in mortification.

A short while later, peace and harmony and a growing feeling of excitement reigned throughout the loft. Cooler heads were definitely prevailing, though none, of course, were quite as cool as the little black puppet head that resided on top of the refrigerator flashing that heartfelt human smile you rarely see around New York these days.

I'd taken Rambam step by step through the events in Chicago, and he seemed quite impressed with my insight in divining the parallels between my own experience and that of Jabez Wilson in the Red-Headed League. He seemed troubled when I explained the roles I believed Polly Price and McGovern were playing in the whole sordid affair. Most of all, he appeared to appreciate the linkage I felt had been established between Al Capone, Leaning Jesus, and the kid, who, of course, was McGovern, though he was much too large to be appropriately labeled as such today,

151

even if he often acted like one. Most important, Rambam seemed to understand the gravity of the case and where I was going with it, from one private investigator to another.

"I've got a more practical idea," said Rambam, after I'd brought him up to speed on the investigation. "Why don't the two of us just saddle up and go out in search of the Lost Dutchman's Mine?"

"This could be bigger."

"This could be a bigger pain in the ass."

"Everyone from Eliot Ness to Geraldo Rivera would love to be in our shoes."

"As long as they don't try to get in our pants."

"I'm serious, Rambam."

"That's what I was afraid of. Look, I'll go along with this for two reasons. One, you're my friend. And two, it does have some entertainment value. But there's not one shred of real evidence for what you're suggesting, and there are other more mundane, but far more likely possibilities."

"Such as."

"Such as Polly Price likes McGovern. Maybe your ego can't accept that she fell for his not inconsiderable Irish charm. He's not my type, but who knows? Maybe the two of them just decided to take off for Atlantic City for a few days."

"It is difficult to imagine, but I suppose it's possible."

"Of course it's possible. And it's also possible that your Red-Headed League scenario is just a big red-headed herring. Maybe these two investigations are not related, and neither of them is going very well for you and you've made the classic mistake that amateur private investigators often fall prey to. You've tried to combine two as of yet unsuccessful efforts into one grandiose, self-concocted scheme."

"All right, let's go over to McGovern's and find out."

"I'll go along with you that far, but unless there are seven bullet-riddled members of the O'Bannion Gang lying on McGovern's living-room floor, I'm going to have a hard time believing Al Capone's got anything to do with this."

"Would you go for seven days of dirty laundry?" I said as the two of us headed for the door.

Chapter Thirty-Eight

I knew something was terribly wrong from the very moment Rambam and I had broken and entered McGovern's apartment. For one thing, it was clean and neat as a pin. In all the time I'd known McGovern I'd never seen the place to rise above the level of total disorder. He'd always contended that he had a system for finding things, and quite possibly he did, but no one in the civilized world had ever been able to decipher what it was. Now the place was so clean, spotless, and well ordered you could eat Chicken McGovern off the floor. It looked like the model apartment the realtor sometimes shows to prospective buyers. But I, for one, wasn't buying it. Somebody had been through this place with a methodical vengeance. Somebody who was looking for something.

"Notice anything wrong with the picture?" I said to Rambam as we viewed the neatly stacked piles of newspapers and anal-retentive bookcases and closets.

"Yeah," said Rambam. "The place usually looks like shit."

"At least McGovern's not as big a slob as Ratso," I said.

"That's because *nobody's* as big a slob as Ratso. Okay, so somebody's been through here. Maybe McGovern hired one of those Beverly Hills mobile maid services where fourteen Guatemalan women jump out of a van and clean your house in eleven seconds."

"Or," I said, "he might've just had Hercule Poirot over for a few days as a housepest."

"I'll admit," said Rambam, "that when McGovern's place looks this neat it's comparable to any normal person's place being tossed. But that hardly establishes your Al Capone connection."

"That notion was set in motion by the MIBs."

"McGovern's an MIB?"

"No. McGovern's an MIT."

"Which is?"

"Man in Trouble."

"That's for sure. Now what's an MIB?"

"MIB stands for the mysterious Men in Black who routinely show up to presumably investigate after a UFO sighting."

Rambam looked at me as if I were a prime candidate for the Bandera Home for the Bewildered. As with many Americans, the abstract often became too abstract for him. He wanted some hard evidence and I could see that he was running out of charm.

"You've heard of UFOs," I said. "Unidentified Federal Organizations?"

"I've had dealings with almost all of them, and sooner or later they all turn into MIBs and you wind up an MIT. If you're lucky."

"How can you tell if you're dealing with one of them? It feels like I've been for the past few weeks. Large invisible tentacles and testicles are waiting for me around every corner."

"They are large mammals," said Rambam, as he made a careful tour of the room, stopping near the window by the fire escape. "But they do sometimes leave little tracks in the snow for the discerning eye. Is this the fire escape where McGovern saw his MIB?"

"McGovern's been seeing a lot of MIBs lately. That's why he's an MIT. But yes, that's the fire escape. Why do you ask, Chief Inspector?"

But Rambam did not answer. He appeared to be staring through the curtains at something in the alley. I waited patiently.

"Holy Christ."

"What is it?"

"I don't believe it."

"What is it?"

I moved closer and saw that he was looking at a peculiar little burned circle in the curtain. I'd never noticed it before, but then, I suppose I could be forgiven. Thin curtains are a bit like freaks or bad automobile accidents. You never really look at them so much as you look through them.

"Does McGovern smoke?" asked Rambam grimly as he squatted down to take a better look. The marking was about at scrotum level.

"He hasn't smoked in years," I said.

Rambam continued to examine the thing. Then he gazed up at the building across the alleyway.

"Of course, he probably hasn't changed these curtains in years either," I said.

But Rambam wasn't listening. His face had

taken on a very serious, intense countenance. He stood up again.

"Do you know what caused this burned place on the curtain?" he said, gesturing toward the window.

I took another look at the small spot. The burned place, or whatever it was, appeared to be not dissimilar to the kind of marking you might leave on the curtain if you aimed a cigarette at an upward angle and gently grazed the fabric just enough to barely burn through it.

"How the hell do I know what caused it?" I said. "A midget with a long cigarette holder."

"That's very funny, Kinky, but unless I'm very far off base this curtain was not burned from the inside. And, as you can see, there's a window behind it that probably remains closed most of the time. And there's not even room for a midget with a long cigarette holder to get between the curtain and the glass."

"So where does that leave us?"

"With a laser."

"A laser?"

"You wanted a UFO," said Rambam. "Now you've got one."

Chapter Thirty-Nine

It was getting dark by the time Rambam and I ankled it up Jane Street to Eighth Avenue and navigated our way to the fourth floor of the building across the alley behind McGovern's place. Rambam had narrowed what he felt was the laser site to two apartments with windows opening onto the alley side of the building. He knocked on the

156

door of the first apartment.

"What are we looking for?" I asked, as the door swung open to reveal a happy homosexual couple just sitting down to a romantic candlelit dinner.

"Not this," he said.

We walked down the hall a bit until we came to the door of the other apartment Rambam felt could be a candidate for the laser site. I was beginning to have my doubts about the whole deal.

"What does a laser do anyway?" I said.

"If shot properly onto the window of an apartment like McGovern's, it'll pick up vibrations that can go directly to a computer or be taped and later taken over to a lab."

"And I take it they can glean something from these vibrations?"

"Glean, my ass," said Rambam. "They could've been listening to every fart, belch, and, possibly more importantly, every word that's been spoken in that apartment for the past month."

Rambam knocked on the door and somewhere in the back of my mind a door opened. If McGovern's place had been bugged by a laser, it would explain a lot of things. Whoever was behind the whole setup would've heard McGovern talking to me on a number of occasions, both on the phone and in person. They'd have heard that the great detective, myself, of course, had taken McGovern on as a client. They'd have heard us discuss Leaning Jesus. They'd have known I was going to Chicago.

Rambam knocked on the door again.

Nothing.

"Two B & E's in one evening," he said. "It's not my record, but it ain't bad. Let's just hope there's a laser operation behind this door."

"It'd be quite a letdown," I said, "if all we find in here's a midget with a long cigarette holder walking around burning people's curtains."

"There'd be one less midget," said Rambam grimly, as he started to work on the door.

"You wouldn't pick on somebody half your size, would you?" I said, as the door came open.

"If this is what I think it is," said Rambam, "it's very, very big."

"That's what she told me last night," I said to the back of his head as we entered the apartment.

The place was dark and smelled of dust and disuse. Then Rambam hit the lights and I saw something that seemed out of place. In fact, I saw many things that seemed out of place. Most of the furniture in the place appeared to be jammed into the hallway between the front door and the living room.

"This is what they do," said Rambam, as we performed a two-man country line dance in between a chest of drawers, several table lamps on the floor, and a rocking chair for a child. It could've been for a midget but I now realized the midget wasn't here. Whatever was here, I didn't think I was much going to like.

"They find an apartment," Rambam was saying, "where they know that the occupants have gone on a photo safari to Botswana for seven months and they move the equipment in for the time of the operation. By the time the people who live here get back, everything'll be just like it was when they left. They're very good at this."

"Who's they?"

Rambam didn't answer. He'd emerged from the clutter in the little hallway and was now moving like a power walker toward the window. As I rounded the turn myself, I saw that the living room was entirely bare of furnishings.

"Holy Christ," said Rambam.

"What?"

"Look."

He was pointing at the wooden floor by the window, which featured a fairly solid coat of dust, broken only by three dark smudge spots directly in front of the glass.

"Laser tripod," he said.

"I'd recognize the tracks anywhere."

"This window also provides perfect access to McGovern's apartment."

"Is it possible that there are other explanations for these smudges on the floor?"

"Of course," said Rambam, "but there's no other possible explanation for this little item."

Just against the nearby wall was a small sleek black object that looked dangerously similar to the common ballpoint pen. He picked it up, glanced confirmationally at it, and handed it to me. It read:

U.S. Government
Skilcraft

"You've seen the tracks of the monster," said Rambam. "That's the droppings."

"I just want to live long enough," I said, as I looked across to McGovern's innocent little apartment, "to see technology fail."

"When it does, I'll fax your E-mail."

We both got out of there a lot faster than we'd gotten in. Paranoia, I suppose, had begun to raise its large, ugly head. It was clear to both of us that there was a UFO involved along with lots of MIBs. We hailed a hack on Eighth Avenue and headed uptown. Polly Price's penthouse might provide some more answers, I thought. I told Rambam about the special elevator to the penthouse and the large number of doormen, and he said no problem. I didn't ask any questions. In the B & E department, Rambam was king.

"So who were those masked men?" I said, checking out the cab driver before I spoke. He was an Israeli, but he didn't look like he worked for Mossad.

"Process of elimination," said Rambam. "NYPD doesn't have this kind of equipment. DEA doesn't have the manpower to monitor a little place like McGovern's apartment unless they have good reason to suspect a hundred thousand kilos are moving through it every hour on the hour, which they don't. The CIA has no authority over internal matters unless they have good reason to suspect terrorism is involved, which they don't. That leaves the good ol' FBI."

"Which, from your warm tone of voice, I gather is your least favorite."

"You could throw in the KGB," he said, "and it'd still be my least favorite."

I felt a slight shiver as I watched the grimy, neon New York night slide by my window. There had to be safer places to be. More practical things to do with my life. I meditated on the subject for about twenty blocks, and the only two possibilities that came to mind were starting up a kosher nudist ranch in Texas or being the friend that Janis Joplin never had.

So I sat back with a slight shiver as I watched the grimy, neon New York night slide by my window.

Chapter Forty

"Maybe," said Rambam, as we got out of the hack, "you ought to start thinking about a less dangerous, less stressful line of work. You could settle down with that tattooed lady you were telling me about. Where's she from?"

"San Diego."

"Does she have any kids?"

"Yeah. One boy. Ten years old."

"Well, Kinky, are you prepared to be a stepfather?"

"I'm prepared to be a stepladder," I said.

"Good," said Rambam. "We may need you to get us into this penthouse."

We took a casual Upper West Side walk around the premises to get ourselves acclimated to the situation. The doormen were swarming along the sidewalk and street in front of Polly Price's building. With their snappy uniforms, it looked like either the circus or the Prussian army had come to town, and I wasn't a fan of either one of them. The only army I believed in was the Salvation Army. As far as the circus was concerned, I had three reasons for disliking it. One, my own life had become such a circus lately that I didn't really need the distraction. Two, all the clowns these days seemed to vaguely resemble John Wayne Gacy. Three, ever since the elephant stomped the trainer, broke away from the circus, and had to be killed by police in Honolulu, I've begun to have my doubts about the big top. The owner of the circus was scratching his head about the elephant, who happened to be a mother elephant, and asking the question of the day: "Why did she do it?" The answer is quite simple really. If you were flown back and forth every day and every night across the world in a hot, stuffy, frightening cargo plane and then paraded in front of thousands of screaming idiots with a stupid tiara stapled to your head, you'd run away from the circus, too. Maybe she was looking for Dumbo. Who knows? There's very little we can do about it, at any rate. Everybody's either running away *from* the circus or running away *with* the circus, and the circus keeps ruthlessly, relentlessly rolling until it superimposes itself upon all of our lives, most of which could've used a little grease paint and peanuts anyway. Occasionally, however, the circus hits a little snag, for example the circus train that derailed recently in Florida. All of the animals survived. The only fatalities were a lion tamer and a clown. Maybe God *does* have a sense of humor. If there is a God.

"How the hell are we going to get past all those doormen?" I said, as we walked farther away from the building.

"You won't even see 'em," said Rambam, as he turned left into a dark alley alongside the building. "Just follow me."

"Into the Valley of Death."

"There's always that possibility."

"I doubt if my number's up yet. I'm not that happy."

"You're not making me very happy either," said Rambam. "I'm used to bucking the odds, but me and you against the FBI isn't anything I'd want any action on."

"Well, as Damon Runyon once said: 'All of life is six to five against.'"

"I wonder if he's ever broken into a penthouse."

"Not lately."

We took another left at the back of the building

and walked over broken glass, trash, and other crap along the not-so-attractive backside of the beautiful building. At last we arrived at a poorly lit, rather dingy door marked: Emergency Exit. If Door Is Opened, Alarm Will Ring.

"Notice that alarm bell in its casing?" said Rambam. "It's the good old-fashioned kind. I'm going to look around back here for a while. Meanwhile, I've got an errand for you."

"Yes, mother."

"You know that drugstore we passed on the corner? Get us a can of shaving cream. Economy size."

"This is no time for practical jokes," I said to the back of Rambam's head, as he walked farther off into the gloom.

I'd already had a couple of pretty close shaves, I thought, as I headed rather grudgingly for the drugstore. Probably, I'd been lucky to get out of Washington and Chicago alive. I'd have to be more careful on future field trips. Maybe these guys hadn't really intended to kill me, but the whole experience wasn't doing much for my mental health. And if you keep messing with somebody, even if they don't want to croak you, they could change their mind. I was certainly changing mine.

What had once seemed like a perfectly straightforward missing person investigation now was pointing the fickle finger of suspicion directly at the person whom once I'd thought of as my client. The frivolous, quirky, nuisance investigation into the goings-on both inside and outside of McGovern's large head had now escalated into what appeared to be shaping up to be a personal confrontation with the Federal Bureau of Investigation. And on top of all that, McGovern could quite conceivably be perched on top of my client right now in some hotel suite while I'm busy here fetching a can of shaving cream for Rambam. Economy size.

It was just like Shoshone the Magic Pony, I reflected, as I put the bag with the can of shaving cream under my arm and called Polly Price's number one more time for good measure from a pay phone on the corner. Nothing in life is what it appears to be. And, as in the case of Polly's telephone, there didn't appear to be any answer. You just had to keep shopping for shaving cream and drinking coffee and following the tedious trail of the bad guys until you couldn't tell the difference between them and everybody else and anyway you didn't give a damn anymore. Maybe you'd find someone who'd been missing. Maybe you'd find what you were looking for. Maybe you thought that you'd been following your star and then one dark, lonely night you looked up and found that it was none of the above.

Just for the hell of it, I dialed the number of my favorite member of New York's finest, Detective Sergeant Mort Cooperman. He wasn't in but his executive butt-boy, Sergeant Buddy Fox, was.

"How lovely to hear from you, Tex," said Fox somewhat facetiously. "Haven't seen you since we found that dead meat in the trunk of that car." He was referring to a lawyer named Hamburger that Kent Perkins and I had indeed found croaked in the trunk of a Lincoln in an underground parking garage.

"I need a quick favor, Sergeant."

"We're here to serve, Tex," he said, in a bored monotone that might've been an indicator of his level of enthusiasm for the project.

164

I gave him Derrick Price's name and the license number of his car. Rambam had already run this information through the DMV and his hard-boiled computer and learned that Derrick Price had stepped on a rainbow seven years before. But rainbows were funny things. They came and they went and not everybody saw them the same way. If Price was who I thought he was, I wanted NYPD's read on this. Not that I thought they'd bust their hump to help me, but their reaction might be interesting.

"We'll jump right on it," said Fox, with a smirk I could almost hear. "Priority one, for sure."

I started to thank him, but he'd already hung up. So I took the bag with the shaving cream back to Rambam, who'd managed to cut a little hole in the bell casing and now proceeded to fill the insides with enough lather to shave and groom every poodle in Central Park. Then he opened the door to a barely audible buzz that sounded more like a bee than a bell.

"So much for building security," he said, as the two of us stepped quickly into the dank basement.

"You know there's a problem here," I said. "The elevator won't take us all the way. You need a special key to take it up to the penthouse."

"No problem," said Rambam. "We're taking the service elevator and I'll bet you anything it isn't rigged with a special key to get us to the penthouse. It's a funny thing, but people who live in penthouses or even plan to visit them would never dream of riding up in a service elevator."

"They probably think it's beneath them," I said, as we wandered down a long dark hallway.

We located the service elevator and I saw that Rambam had been right. We rode all the way up to the penthouse with a cartful of dirty linen. Moments later, Rambam was working on Polly Price's penthouse door, his third B & E of the night—fourth, if you wanted to count the building's emergency exit. Maybe one alarm bell had been muted, but another had started to sound somewhere in the back of my own penthouse, and somehow I didn't believe shaving cream was going to silence it. It was a voice, actually. Far away, frantic, and frighteningly familiar.

It said: "MIT! MIT! MIT!"

Chapter Forty-One

Polly Price's penthouse proved to be a more daunting adversary for Rambam than McGovern's apartment or the spy nest across the alley. After a full five minutes of knocking, ringing the bell, and Rambam's having taken from his pockets virtually every device known to man for getting oneself on the other side of a locked door, we were still standing in the hallway.

"What do we do?" I said. "We can't stand here forever."

"Grab a mop," said Rambam. "Be a janitor."

"What," I said, "and give up show business?"

"Especially when we're getting ready for our big opening," said Rambam, as he extracted a strange-looking device from his pocket. The thing resembled a small flashlight with a prong-type mechanism on one end of it.

"What the hell is that?"

"Electric lockpick. It was developed by the feds. The probe on the end vibrates about one thousand times a minute."

"I imagine female federal agents are very fond of it."

"If we ever see your client again, we can ask her," said Rambam, as he inserted the dingus into the keyhole and turned on the switch.

The operation was over very quickly. The whole thing required just about as much time as it takes for a heart to break. Rambam turned the knob and the door swung open silently. He held out his hand magnanimously for me to enter.

"Age before experience," he said.

"Fools before angels," I said, holding back.

"She's your client," said Rambam.

"Okay," I said, "watch my back."

"Not if there's anything else on."

I entered the foyer of the penthouse with Rambam close behind me. The place was dark and silent as a tomb. I had by now come to the firm conclusion that the fine feminine hand of Polly Price was behind a great deal of my recent aggravation. I felt fairly certain that she'd been interested in McGovern long before she'd even known of my existence. As for Derrick Price, finding him was about as likely as Jesus coming back as the Easter Bunny.

I was listening for a moment and letting my eyes adjust to the gloom when Rambam turned on the lights.

"So much for letting our eyes adjust to the darkness," I said.

"Adjust away," said Rambam. "There's nothing to see. So let there be light."

"And the Lord said: 'This sucks.'"

Indeed it did. The place had been totally cleaned out. An empty penthouse in an empty world. All that remained were the chandeliers and, I noticed as we walked out on the balcony, the strange piece of sculpture upon which I'd not so long ago louvered my buttocks.

"Don't sit on that," I said. "It's a piece of art."

"And your client's a piece of work," said Rambam, as he wandered back along the empty hallways.

"What client?" I said.

"What client is right. Forget about finding her. The beast covers its tracks too well. We could search for the rest of our lives and never find a trace of them. Never be sure what they were really up to."

"What do we do about finding McGovern?"

"We just hope he comes home," said Rambam, "wagging his tail behind him."

"Some tail," I said.

"Some home," said Rambam.

We decided to leave the building through the front entrance and as we walked across the lavish lobby we encountered yet another surprise. One of the doormen came running up to us in a state of mild excitement.

"Mr. Friedman! Mr. Friedman!" he said. "I just came on my shift. I didn't see you come in."

"I thought I'd come in the emergency exit," I said. "I figured if I filled the bell full of shaving cream nobody'd get alarmed."

I laughed. Rambam laughed. The doorman, whose name tag read "Carlos," laughed. I'd never seen the man before in my life.

"That's a good joke, Mr. Friedman," said Carlos, continuing to laugh. Some Latin cultures tend to find more humor than many situations often merit.

"He's a killer," agreed Rambam.

"How did you know my name, Carlos?" I said.

"Miss Price left an envelope for you. She said if a man with a big black cowboy hat comes in here smoking a big cigar, give him this envelope."

Carlos handed me the envelope. "Mr. Friedman" had been typed on the front. The envelope was sealed.

"Where is Miss Price now?" I asked.

"Miss Price," said Carlos, shrugging his shoulders extravagantly, "she's gone away."

"You can say that again," said Rambam.

I thanked Carlos, and we walked outside, past the phalanx of doormen and down the sidewalks of New York. I stopped under a streetlamp and opened the envelope and read Polly Price's brief letter to me. Then I handed it to Rambam and he read it and handed it back to me.

The note read:

You're a nice man, Kinky Friedman. In another time and another place, who knows? I'll never forget you.

Love,
Polly

"You really have a way with women," said Rambam.

Chapter Forty-Two

Like a childhood accordion collapsing, all the air seemed to have gone out of the case at once. I admit to mostly feeling a pervading sense of relief as we walked along the thoroughfares of the Upper West Side. Trendy places were everywhere, of-

ten right next door to more authentic places populated by last year's people. I liked last year's people,
I decided. But then, I suppose, I always had. I
could live without ever seeing Polly Price again,
without even ever knowing exactly what her game
was. As far as her retainer went, which wasn't all
that far considering what I'd recently been
through, I could just hang on to the money or
earmark it for some worthy charity. For the Benefit of Mr. Kite sounded about right.

The only dark cloud on my horizon now, and it
was a rather large one, was the curious absence of
McGovern. He was very indestructible, very loyal,
and very stubborn, but he was also, I reflected
with a glint of guilt, very vulnerable. I just didn't
know where to take it from here. The trail, if that's
what it indeed was, had come to an end. Not for
the first time in my life, I'd hitched my wagon to a
falling star, and now I simply wished that
McGovern would come safely back home.

Rambam seemed subdued and introspective
himself as we walked along Amsterdam to 87th
Street and stood outside of Barney Greengrass,
one of the oldest and greatest delis in New York.

"Joel Siegel took me here years ago," I said.
"The place is really killer bee."

"Lox specialist to the world," said Rambam.
"Too bad it's closed."

"Like the Polly Price file."

"Just as well," said Rambam. "Messing with the
FBI is like taking a picture of an Indian. Every
time you do it it sucks out a little bit more of your
soul."

We walked around the corner to a little bar that
was open and found an empty table and ordered
a round.

"Obviously," I said, "the feds were using me to learn more about McGovern. Now that they've got McGovern, they don't need me. And for all the enormous amount of effort, expenditures, and subterfuge they involved themselves with, it's got to be something big they're after."

"Like what?"

"Like the same thing Geraldo Rivera thought he'd find when he went into what he hoped was Al Capone's secret vault on live television."

"The money and manpower the feds put into something has nothing to do with anything. Look at what they did a few years back to Randy Weaver, the survivalist in Idaho who lived in an isolated cabin and was guilty of the heinous crime of selling someone a gun of a prohibited length. They spent about ten million dollars, killed Weaver's son, dog, and then shot and killed his wife as she stood in the cabin doorway with her baby in her arms. They weren't looking for Al Capone's treasure. They weren't really looking for anything. They were just a deadly, mindless swarm of hornets somebody'd stirred up. I don't want you to be another Randy Weaver."

"They did a nice job recently in Waco, too."

"And those are just the ones everybody knows about," said Rambam, warming to the subject. "J. Edgar Hoover ran that outfit like an American Gestapo for almost five decades, and believe me, since the bastard croaked it hasn't changed all that much. Hoover was a vicious anti-Semite as well as a fag basher, even though he and his lifelong companion, Clyde Tolson, were closet queens the whole fucking time and I do mean the whole fucking time."

"Can I push your stool in for you?"

Rambam ignored my effort at lightening the mood. He continued his clinical recall on the evils of the FBI, stopping only to order another round.

"Hoover burgled the offices of a lot of Jewish organizations. He had a room called the Jew Room loaded with files on prominent Jews from all walks of life. He believed all Jews were either spies or communists."

"He forgot doctors."

"The FBI was the home of the original dirty-tricks boys long before Nixon ever had his first erection. They burgled Dustin Hoffman's shrink's office and stole his private files to help protect America. They spent millions of taxpayer dollars and man hours hounding and harassing and spying on dangerous enemies of our country like John Lennon, Leonard Bernstein, Arthur Miller, and Martin Luther King."

"Don't forget Burl Ives."

"Burl Ives? How'd you know that?"

"The Friedman of Information Act."

"Okay," said Rambam, pausing in his monologue to chuckle briefly. "Burl Ives. Where was I?"

"Hoover and the Hebes."

"Right. The FBI tried to foment trouble and dissension between Abbie Hoffman and Jerry Rubin by sending phony letters and starting false rumors in a campaign of disinformation worthy of the KGB—"

"A little piece of spiritual trivia," I said. "Did you know that Jerry Rubin's death certificate lists his occupation as 'Jewish Road Warrior?'"

"That's one of the things they all had in common. A huge number of people the FBI hounded were Jewish."

"Not Burl Ives."

"Okay, Kinky. Not Burl Ives."

"Not Martin Luther King either."

"I won't argue that one. But what they did to him was really amazing. Martin Luther King was given to fooling around a bit, apparently, in his extramarital area. So these fuckers pursued him relentlessly and got his whole life on tape. They'd bug his hotel rooms when he was on the road and come up with some gem like: 'Oh, Martin, your dick is so big!' Then they'd call his wife and play the tape into the phone. They'd get some white agent to imitate a black accent—they didn't have any black agents back then—and he'd do a half-assed Amos 'n' Andy impersonation. Say something like: 'Miss King, I wants to play you this tape out of concern. Looks like your husband's in Wisconsin and he's brought along his johnson.' Then they'd play her the tape: 'Oh, Martin, your dick is so big!' That's the kind of shit the FBI did."

"Then God punished J. Edgar Hoover," I said. "He gave Martin Luther King a holiday and he didn't give J. Edgar Hoover dick."

"And that's what he'd always wanted. Of course, by that time, Martin Luther King was probably ready for a holiday."

I was ready for another shot of Old Grand-Dad and I decided to try a Guinness to back it up. It was an interesting combination and it was starting to give me a little buzz. Rambam was dipping his nose into some kind of obscure, very expensive brandy that smelled like somebody's feet. I didn't know what it tasted like, but it had Rambam rolling along full throttle on the FBI.

"Another thing. They have about nine thousand agents in the field. Multiplying like rabbits with very big ears every time you turn around. And

173

they never let them work in the area they're from. This is different from cops. Cops live in a neighborhood, raise families there. They know the people. They want to retire there usually. But the feds are different. They parachute them in from as far away as possible. So you got a fed from Alabama and they put him in New York and he's walking around among all these strange-looking, foreign-sounding people, orthodox Jews, Puerto Ricans, Orientals, and he hates everybody and comes to see himself as an enemy force. He wants to fuck *everybody*.

"I've had personal experience with the feds, too. They came to me once and wanted me to help them with some murder investigation they were working on. I met with them a few times and came to the conclusion they were going after the wrong guy. So I told them what I thought and that, under the circumstances, I wouldn't be able to help. That didn't go down very well with them. So they sent agents to talk to my landlord, my clients, my friends and they said 'We'd like to talk to you about Rambam. It's in connection with a murder investigation.' Well, when the FBI comes to you and says something like that, you immediately jump to the conclusion that Rambam is the murderer. My landlord freaked. I lost clients. My friends were all calling wondering what the hell was going on. And once that kind of damage is done it's hard to undo."

"Ask Randy Weaver."

"At least I didn't have a wife, a kid, and a dog. All they managed to do was to temporarily destroy my reputation."

"Which wasn't the best when they started."

"The point is, I've been through a hell of a lot

of shit with the FBI and never again do I want to have anything to do with them. I've worked *with* them and I've worked *against* them and I definitely prefer against. Of course the Secret Service are pretty good guys. Unless you're goin' after the President."

"Okay, so what do we do about McGovern?"

"If he's in the clutches of the feds, there's nothing we can do about it. They'll get what they want from him—if they even know what they want—and then they'll let him go. He'll be okay. Besides, look at the positive side of the situation."

"What's that?"

"Somebody finally cleaned up his apartment."

Chapter Forty-Three

I couldn't sleep that night, but it wasn't because I was lonely. After having listened to Rambam's oral dissertation on the FBI, I had my doubts if I'd ever feel lonely again. Or alone, for that matter. As I paced back and forth across the living room of the loft, smoking a cigar, listening to the lesbian dance class overhead, I wondered if somebody else wasn't listening, too. Maybe somebody had tapes of my conversations with the cat. Maybe somebody besides myself and God knew that Stephanie DuPont took three showers a day. Everything Rambam said, of course, was not the gospel. The FBI, no doubt, had performed many good and valorous acts for this country over the years. The problem was that also over the years, great power had accrued to the organization, most of it centered in one man, J. Edgar Hoover. If power tends to corrupt, it didn't have far to go with old J. Edgar. He spied with an iron hand on anyone who had ideas different from his own. And he set the standard for the mentality of the FBI agent to be a control addict.

Like taking pictures of an Indian, Rambam had said. Somebody was watching Arthur Miller who never would appreciate *Death of a Salesman*. Another somebody was closely monitoring John Lennon. Somebody who could never imagine "Imagine." And the whole world remembers Martin Luther King for "I have a dream." Only J. Edgar Hoover and his pathetic acolytes would remember him for "Oh, Martin, your dick is so big!" Maybe that was what Hoover had really wanted all along.

I went over to the desk and dialed McGovern's number. I got no answer. I'd called him four or five times already this night and always I'd gotten no answer. Always I'd hung up the blower and walked over to the bottle of Jameson on the counter. Always I'd poured a shot into the old bull's horn and fired it straight at my uvula. Always the cat had watched with thinly veiled disgust in her eyes.

"I miss McGovern," I said.

The cat said nothing. She did not miss McGovern. She did not miss anybody. I looked closely into her roulette eyes and for a moment I wasn't even sure if she missed me when I was away from the loft. Maybe that was the way to be. Cold-blooded. Protect yourself. That was fine, unless you were the Indian someone was taking pictures of. Unwanted visions of McGovern's clean apartment ransacked my mind. Were they holding him prisoner somewhere? Interrogating him? Giving him lie-detector tests? Shooting him up with truth

serum like they do in spy movies? Could whatever Leaning Jesus had given him be that important to anyone? And why did McGovern insist he
couldn't remember what it was? Just tell them,
McGovern. Get it over with. Otherwise they'll
hound you to your grave. If they don't decide to
put you in it first.

At three o'clock in the morning, dressed in my
Borneo batik sarong and old purple bathrobe, I
found myself standing at the kitchen window looking out on Vandam Street as I had done many
weeks ago on New Year's Day, the day Hank Williams had died. That was before I'd met Polly Price.
Before I'd taken the bait to find her missing husband. Before I'd gone to Washington. Before I'd
gone to Chicago. Unfortunately, I didn't know a
hell of a lot more now than I had then. All I knew
was that the world outside the window looked
cold. Colder than a cold, cold heart.

I was smoking a Cuban cigar as I gazed numbly
into the frozen darkness, sipping a cup of Hawai-
ian coffee, half-consciously stroking the cat on the
windowsill. Business as usual. My mind was still
at work. In its troubled, churning, confused state
it was processing the recent past, looking for an
answer from a world that didn't give a damn.

In many ways, I reflected, as I watched the tail-
lights of a taxi vanish into the gloom, this had been
one of my least satisfying cases. In fact, the Derrick Price investigation, much to my chagrin, had
probably never really been a case at all. A bad joke
was more like it. A red herring on an endless loop.
A charade. A facade. A shadow game. A well-
timed, trivial, rather tedious treasure hunt.

I looked in the cat's eyes and caught a glimmer
from a car's headlights somewhere down the street,

shyly shining like the moon reflects the sun. Maybe there was a treasure after all, I thought. Maybe Leaning Jesus had never revealed to McGovern the precise nature of the gift he had given him. Maybe it was something that a person would never think of as important. Maybe, just maybe, all this time, McGovern had the map to the Lost Dutchman's Mine and hadn't even known it.

The certitude that I now seemed to feel about the existence of this treasure, for no good reason at all, was suddenly making me feel rather fey. For those of you who don't believe in leprechauns, fey is a word of Irish derivation that has about as many shades of meaning as there are colors in the rainbow. It can mean "enchanted," "clairvoyant," or "in touch with the higher powers." It can also mean "in touch with the fairies," or "in touch with the leprechauns." It could also mean, I thought hopefully, in touch with McGovern, who, though ridiculously large for a leprechaun, shared a great many of their behavioral and character traits.

But, as my kid sister, Marcie, sometimes delights in pointing out, there is yet another definition for the word "fey." It is somewhat less well known in terms of usage, and, of course, it is not particularly the kind of emotion you'd want to possess if you can help it. Fey can also mean "to feel inexplicably happy before impending doom or, possibly, death."

I did not intend to discuss the shades of meaning of the word "fey" with the cat at this or any other time. Cats are not Irish. They are usually French, Jewish, or Siamese. Dogs, however, are almost invariably Irish, with a few notable exceptions such as my father's dog, Sambo, who has been well-documented to be a Jewish Shepherd.

Nonetheless, I attempted to share my feelings with the cat.

"I feel strangely hopeful," I said, "for no reason at all. But it feels like somebody might come along and pull the rug out from under me at any moment."

I looked around at the no man's land outside the window, the mildly bored cat, the stark, almost impersonal, gloom-gathering living room. There wasn't even a rug for somebody to come along and pull out. I walked over to the percolator and poured a new head onto my semi-luke coffee. In my old head, however, the same old thoughts seemed to be percolating, like little coffee grinds of doubt ebbing and flowing with the tide almost invisibly across the black sand beaches of some Kona of the heart. I could almost feel the fey slipping away. Yet I vowed to remain upbeat, if only for the cat.

"Before we can look for the treasure," I said, "first we've got to find McGovern."

With an expression of supreme disbelief bordering upon exasperation in her eyes, the cat gazed up at the ceiling where Winnie Katz and her lesbian dance troupe were, thankfully, silent, whatever that portended. Then the cat turned and padded without guilt or hesitation into the bedroom wherein she gracefully leaped upon the bed and curled up into what appeared to be the instantaneous slumber of the innocent. It was clearly one of the reasons, I reflected in the kitchen window, why many people hated cats.

It's a cold, uncaring world we live in, I thought. And that's in the best of times. Nobody had heeded McGovern's frantic and persistent MIB reports. Even his closest friends, I remembered with a pang of guilt, had deigned to turn a deaf ear. Hell, nobody would believe me now if I tried to tell them what I thought to be the truth. Not the cops. Not the newspapers. Not the cat.

I stared out into the New York nothingness that was not dark and not dawn but possibly only the mere absence of the human spirit.

"God bless you, J. Edgar Hoover," I said grimly to myself. "You're the only one who listens anymore."

Chapter Forty-Four

"It's been five days since Rambam and I broke into his apartment," I said, "and he's still not back."

"Maybe it's something as simple as boy meets girl," said Stephanie DuPont.

"Kind of like us."

"Don't make me sick, Friedman."

In the low, romantic lighting of the little Indian restaurant in the East Village, she looked, if possible, more radiant and ravishing than ever. Two weeks of helicopter skiing in Switzerland certainly hadn't hurt the girl. Not that I especially knew what helicopter skiing was. I did not have a particular fondness for skiing or for helicopters or for Switzerland, for that matter. But I did have a particular fondness for Stephanie DuPont.

"Look," I said patiently, "I've told you everything that's happened since you've been gone and surely you've reached the conclusion that Polly Price is not just a girl. She's a federal agent. Possibly worse. She may be some kind of counterespionage rogue terrorist—"

180

"Waiter," said Stephanie sweetly. "Please bring my father some of those little cheese balls for dessert."

"And the boy didn't meet the girl," I continued, unruffled. "The girl arranged through my good offices a method of gaining his confidence and then proceeded to seduce him in order to find out about Leaning Jesus."

"We're not sounding a little jealous, are we?"

"The only ones I'm jealous of are Pyramus and Thisbe."

"I *told* you I'm making a leash for you," said Stephanie, in a voice a little louder than necessary. A number of our fellow diners looked over with gazes of mildly prurient interest. "By the way, your face is now the color of mulligatawny soup. I'm warning you, Friedman. Don't push me. I'm only twenty-two. Let me grow up. I'm just a kid."

"Tell that to the guy at the far table whose turban just popped off."

I poured us both another glass of Taj Mahal beer, which comes in a bottle a little larger and almost the same shape as an old-fashioned wooden bowling pin. When you drink three or four of them it feels like you've been hit over the head by an old-fashioned wooden bowling pin. But the vindaloo dishes tend to work like a spicy culinary form of speed and you don't get as heavily monstered as you might've. Usually.

"I'm telling you," I said, "if McGovern's not back or I haven't heard from him by the end of this weekend I'm going to the cops. I'll tell 'em the whole story. I'll file a missing person report."

"Don't make me laugh," said Stephanie with mild disgust. "They'll never believe you."

"But *you* believe me," I said, giving her the best

181

searching stare I currently had in stock.

"Of course," said Stephanie. "Not even you could dream up anything this crazy. Let me see if I have it. About a zillion years ago, as the ice was melting in God's cocktail glass—"

"It wasn't so long ago," I explained. "Much of what happened transpired in my lifetime."

"As I was saying," said Stephanie, "about a zillion years ago, as the ice was melting in God's cocktail glass, Al Capone hops off to prison and before he goes, gives his executive butt-boy, Leaning Jesus, a letter or a document or a map that details where he's stashed all the loot he's plundered in all the years he's been king of the mob. When the feds make things hot for Leaning Jesus, he, for safekeeping, dutifully transfers said document to young Mike McGovern—"

"You *will* make a good lawyer—"

"—who not only can't find said document but can't even remember receiving it. How'm I doing so far?"

"Right on the money, as it were."

"Okay. Now in sixty-eight, McGovern moves to New York, where he works as a journalist and lives a lifestyle not calculated to help improve his retrieval system, not to mention twenty-seven fun-filled years passing by. Longer than some of us have been alive."

"Don't rub it in. So I'm young at heart."

"You're not young at heart. You're young at dick. All men are."

"Your sexism appalls me."

"Then sometime during my happy, carefree childhood—"

"—which is still in progress—"

"—some feds or ex-feds or former feds along

182

with Geraldo Rivera and half the civilized, as well as the uncivilized, world begin to put out their feelers for whatever happened to all of Al Capone's bucks. Nobody finds the mother lode, but maybe some informer squeals, or some old field agent retires with some classified documents and finally manages to connect the dots between Al Capone, Leaning Jesus, and Mike McGovern."

"I'd like to connect the dots on this credit-card voucher," I said, putting on my reading skepticals. "The check appears to be written in Aramaic."

"So this cell, or whatever it is, now proceeds to closely monitor McGovern's every move, throwing in as well a campaign of harassment and threats that is making him crazy so he turns to you, who, as we well know, already are crazy."

"Nobody called me bad names at the hospital."

"So now, through the wonders of modern technology, every word that transpires between you and McGovern, whether in person or over the phone, is being picked up by these people and so some of the surveillance spills over onto you. They get you to put one of their people in personal contact with McGovern. They devise ways to get you out of town and comb your loft. They find nothing, so they decide, What the hell, let's let Friedman lead us to Leaning Jesus, which in time you do."

"How stupid of me."

"Careless is a better word."

"Thank you, Miss Marple."

"So now you and Rambam are running around after the fact with satellite dishes on your heads trying to jam their signals or something and meanwhile they have McGovern."

"Which is about like having a Ouija board. But I'm hoping he knows more than he knows he knows. Memories are funny little things. You haven't had time to really have a lot of them yet. At twenty-two, you probably know more now than you ever will again."

Stephanie almost sulked, but I could see she was thinking about it. Then she looked at me with the sudden eyes of a child. It was like watching a brooding buttermilk sky just as it clears to be breathtaking, flag-waving, lovemaking, Texas summer blue.

"Don't worry," she said consolingly. "They won't hurt McGovern. He'll come back and then you can talk to him. Find out what it is that he doesn't know or what he has that he doesn't know he has. Your mind may be gone, but you have a brilliant imagination. Use it. You can still be my hero, you know."

"What do I have to do? Fit my scrotum through the eye of a needle?"

Stephanie laughed a loud, primitive, somehow sensuous laugh. I poured us both the last of the Taj Mahal.

"No, Long Dong Sliver," she said. "Just find Al Capone's secret treasure."

Chapter Forty-Five

The weekend passed slowly, like rush-hour traffic of the mind. My mind was jammed with thoughts and concerns about McGovern. Both Rambam and Stephanie had predicted he'd be back before I knew it, but I wasn't buying anything retail. Where was McGovern? What were they doing to him? Why hadn't he at least called? For some reason, I felt more like a mother than a friend. Since McGovern's own mother had stepped on a rainbow some years ago, possibly the role had devolved to me.

Late Sunday night, throwing all caution to the winds, I decided to call McGovern's live-out girlfriend, Beverly. If it had been a case of boy meets girl, or if it'd started differently and ended up that way, the last thing I wanted to do was alert the war department. On the other hand, McGovern had been missing for almost a week now. If I hadn't heard anything and Beverly hadn't heard anything, it was not a good sign. Our boy had gone from seeing an MIB to being an MIT to becoming an MIA.

Beverly, among other endeavors, had cofounded an acting troupe called Theater for the Forgotten. The purpose of the group was to perform in prisons, mental hospitals, halfway houses for homosexual hatchet murderers, and other places where normal Americans fear to tread. There was always something about the name of her organization that had bothered me, but I never could remember what it was.

"Theater for the Forgotten," I said to the cat. "It's a damn near perfect description of what I've been through lately."

The cat did not seem to care a great deal. For one thing, she'd been ignorant of my trials and tribulations in Washington and Chicago. For another, she had never been enamored of theatrical presentations. She particularly abhorred *Cat on a Hot Tin Roof.*

"You see," I explained, "the entire search for Polly Price's missing husband, as well as much of what McGovern thought was happening to him could be categorized as pure theater. The only thing that's really important is what McGovern has forgotten. Which, of course, raises the question: 'Is the theater really dead?'"

I walked over to the desk, picked up the blower on the left, and dialed Beverly's number in the country, as they say. When you live in New York City, of course, the country is just about everywhere else.

"Kinky," Beverly said, as she pole-vaulted past hello, "have you seen Mike?"

"Never could see Mike. How about yourself?"

"I haven't seen or heard from him in over a week. I'm very worried about Mike, Kinky."

As long as I'd known Beverly, she'd been very worried about Mike. This time, however, I was afraid she might really have something. I didn't want to panic her, but I wasn't exactly filled with the even-mindedness of the old Mahatma myself at the moment.

"You know, Kinky, he's been behaving in a very bizarre and paranoid fashion for several months now."

"Maybe he's practicing to be a New Yorker."

"He hasn't been himself at all lately," Beverly continued, becoming increasingly agitato. "And now he's disappeared! And his apartment's been all cleaned up!"

"That's *really* strange."

"You have no idea where he is?" she said, taking on a mildly interrogative tone.

"That's correct."

"And you have no idea *who* he's with?"

"That's correct," I said, a little too quickly.

The conversation seemed to have run into

something of a wall. I removed the little deerstalker cap from Sherlock's head and extracted a fresh cigar, upon which I began performing fairly Freudian acts with my lips and teeth and tongue. Then I set fire to the cigar with a kitchen match, always keeping the tip of the cigar ever so slightly above the level of the flame.

"Should we go to the police, Kinky?" Beverly was saying, as I blew a plume of smoke up toward the lesbian dance class.

"I'll be calling them first thing tomorrow morning," I said. "And I'll let you know what they say." I could already imagine what they were going to say and it wasn't going to be anything Beverly was going to want to hear. So I gave her a little something to settle her nerves.

"Look," I said, paraphrasing Rambam, "I'm sure he'll come home soon, wagging his tail behind him."

If that were to occur, unfortunately, I didn't think it was going to be the kind of tail that Beverly was going to like to see.

Chapter Forty-Six

The first thing Monday morning turned out to be about twelve forty-five in the afternoon. That was the time I'd taken care of my morning ablutions, had enough cups of espresso to clear Charlotte's Web out of my brain, cleaned up some rather distasteful cat vomit from off my desk, and sat down to call Sergeant Cooperman. For a change, the desk sergeant put me right through.

"Make it fast," said Cooperman. "I'm just leaving for a big, important assignment. It's called lunch."

I told Cooperman that I wanted to file a missing person report on McGovern. It was not easy explaining to him why I was worried about McGovern. First, I had to try to put everything that had happened on a bumper sticker for him. Second, as I related some of the more unusual aspects of the case, I had to attempt not to sound like I needed a checkup from the neck up. By the time I'd finished my Torah portion, it didn't even sound very convincing from my side of the blower.

"You gotta be kiddin'," said Cooperman, halfway between a laugh and a choke. "Your friend McGovern don't sound like he needs a missing person report. You ought to be sending him a bottle of champagne. Any fool can see he's shacking up with that broad."

"I still have a problem with that," I said.

"Yeah," said Cooperman, sounding restless. "What's your problem?"

"Where do I send the champagne?"

"By the way," said Cooperman, dismissing the question entirely, "that plate number you gave Fox the other day for the vehicle supposedly belonging to the guy who was supposedly your client's husband who you were supposedly trying to locate?"

"Yeah?"

"Checks out to be a bread truck in Brooklyn. Now, based on these two parallel investigations you say you've been conducting, I've been able to arrive at a few conclusions of my own."

"Which are?" I said warily.

"McGovern's either bull-fucking your client—"

"Or?"

"He's driving that bread truck."

The last sound I heard before I cradled the

blower was Cooperman either choking to death or chuckling to beat the band. At the moment, I didn't much care which.

The espresso machine seemed to be humming to itself, so I went over and got a cupful and then walked over to the refrigerator and spoke briefly with the puppet head.

"'Education never ends, Watson,'" I said. "'It's a series of lessons with the greatest for the last.'"

The puppet head smiled understandingly.

"But this is not the Red-Headed League. This is not something out of *Treasure Island*. This is New York in the nineties where, all too often, nothing is delivered. Fiction is the ability to imagine and to believe what you have imagined. We like a good mystery because it affords us resolution, something that life itself so rarely does. Now if McGovern ever returns to the city, we can go out and pour a few drinks down our necks and forget it all ever happened."

The puppet head smiled understandingly.

I smiled understandingly.

It wasn't all that hard to understand. Sometimes you win and sometimes you lose and sometimes you live in a lonely loft in February, freezing your ass off, listening to dancing lesbians, gazing at garbage trucks, smoking cigars, drinking espresso, attempting to relate to an antisocial cat, feeling sorry for yourself, and, occasionally, carrying on a rather wooden conversation with a little black puppet head who resides on top of the refrigerator and is the only one with the brains and the guts and the imagination to call this place home.

I walked over to the couch and lay down for a little power nap, pulling Ryan Kalmin's old blue sleeping bag over me for a comforter. I dreamed of Polly Price. Or was it Irene Adler, the woman who bested Sherlock Holmes and revealed that he had a heart by stealing it? It was no coincidence that the bar where Polly had met Ratso was in Washington. She'd gotten what she'd wanted from me. That was McGovern. Now it was just a question of whether or not she could get what she wanted from him.

It must've been a hell of a power nap, because when I opened my eyes the loft was dark and the phones were ringing like church bells after a war. I felt like I'd just been through one myself as I shivered and stumbled my way across the gloomy room to the desk and with an icy dead man's grip, collared the blower on the left.

The voice that came over the wire was upbeat and very familiar, with a decidedly British accent, which, in time, I recognized belonged to Pete Myers.

"Kinkster!" Myers boomed enthusiastically. "McGovern's back! I've got him right here at the shop and he's asking to see you."

"Can you hold him till I get there?"

"It doesn't look like he's planning to go anywhere soon, Kinkster. He's leaning peacefully against the Dikstuffer, smoking a joint, and drinking directly from a bottle of very expensive, very hard to get imported twenty-five-year-old Macallan high-grade straight malt scotch that I was saving for a dinner party later this week."

"I'll pop right over, mate."

I slipped into my blue Oliver Twist coat, put on my cowboy hat, and grabbed three cigars for the road.

I left the cat in charge.

As I hurried down the four flights of stairs I realized, somewhat belatedly, that it really didn't matter who was in charge. There was very damn little left for anyone to be in charge of. McGovern was back. The game was over. The case was closed. I felt a sudden certitude that Polly and her crew had failed to get what they wanted from McGovern. No one ever would. If indeed Leaning Jesus had ever given Capone's papers to the Kid, they'd been strewn somewhere along the pathway from childhood. The Kid no longer existed. He was now, for better or worse, a man. No truth serum, no hypnosis, no casting the mind back would ever recover what had been lost, misplaced, forgotten, or, quite simply, never there.

No hacks were in sight, so I legged it through the cold, darkened streets of the Village. The bad news was that there'd be no winners this time. No happy endings. I thought wistfully of Stephanie DuPont's statuesque form, caustic wit, stunning smile, and heart of gold. No heroes this time, either. No hacks and no heroes. Just God in His penthouse, Satan in the basement, the cat in the loft, me on the street, and the little black puppet head smiling down from on top of the refrigerator. A million years from now, when archaeologists dug doggedly through the tragic and tedious layers of human existence that had once comprised the ancient city of New York, they would no doubt find that little puppet head. Then, as now, men will probably scratch their own heads in amazement and ask the question that no civilization on earth has yet been able to answer: "Why is he smiling?"

Chapter Forty-Seven

It was almost ten bells by the time I sailed up the frozen asphalt river of Hudson Street and pitched anchor at Myers of Keswick. The shop was closed but its proprietor soon responded to my muted tapping on his chamber door.

"How is he?" I said, as Pete took my coat and hung it by the door.

"A sadder but a wiser man," he said. "So am I. That Macallan's scotch runs a hundred and sixty-one dollars a bottle."

"Has he said anything about where he's been or what he's been doing all this time?"

"I think he's been waiting for you."

I followed Pete Myers to the back of the shop and into the little kitchen where McGovern was still reclining against the Dikstuffer pretty much as Myers had described him earlier, except that now the joint was just a roach and the hundred and sixty-one dollars had devalued itself to about eighty dollars and fifty cents. McGovern looked high enough to hook up with the Mir Space Station, but otherwise he appeared to be fine. A sort of sad, wistful smile seemed frozen on his face, vaguely similar, I now realized, to that on the puppet head. Of course, you'd be smiling too if you'd just spent a week with Polly Price.

"How's it going, old bean?" he said.

I threw him an old, unfinished song lyric of mine to sort of lighten the mood and to see what he'd do with it.

"Can't complain, Can't complain,
Ass got bit by a big Great Dane.
Penis run over by a subway train.

Can't complain. Can't complain."

"Same here," said McGovern.

"Do you care to share some of your experiences?" I said. "At least the ones that are family oriented."

"How would I know? I don't have a family."

"You're wrong there, mate," said Myers. "You do have a family. It's just not the family you were born with. Let's face it, McGovern. You're stuck with us."

"So come on, Magoo," I said. "Spit it. Where'd she take you?"

"We decided to take a drive to a lodge she knew somewhere upstate. It was near a little dairy farm community outside the small town of Manlius, New York. We stayed in a very romantic old bungalow and the first couple of days there I thought I'd died and gone to heaven."

"When you die," said Myers, "you won't be going to heaven."

"At first, Polly and I seemed to be a great comfort to each other. She needed an understanding man in her life and I needed a gorgeous social worker who was built like a brick shithouse."

"How poignant," I said. "So you helped each other work through your grief."

"Is that what they're calling it now?" said Myers.

"Polly seemed to be fascinated with my background. She especially loved hearing me tell stories about Leaning Jesus and all the gang in Chicago. She thought of me as some kind of great eyewitness to the lost and colorful past. She felt she was born too late and the only way it could come to life again was through my eyes. Also, her father died when she was very young and I think she saw Leaning Jesus not only as a father figure to me, but also to her as well. My relationship with him became almost an obsession with her."

"Who's Polly?" said Myers.

"Just a girl we used to know," I said.

"She asked me if I had any letters or papers from Leaning Jesus or gifts from him or pictures. She wanted to see him better, to touch him."

McGovern paused to take about a twenty-dollar swig from the bottle of Macallan's high-grade straight malt scotch. He passed it over to me, and I proceeded to further devalue the liquid assets of Myers of Keswick. Pete himself then took a hearty slug from the bottle.

"Sod the bleeding dinner party," he said.

"Then yesterday morning," McGovern continued, as if in a reverie, "I woke up and she was gone. All I found was this note."

He took a crumpled piece of paper from his pocket and handed it to me. I put on my reading skepticals, held the page under a heating lamp, and read the few lines of fine familiar feminine hand:

You're a nice man, Mike McGovern. In another time and another place, who knows? I'll never forget you.

Love,
Polly

P.S. If you see Leaning Jesus before I do just drill a little hole and pull me through.

There was a silence in the little kitchen as Myers read the note and McGovern took another rather expensive pull on the scotch. Then Pete handed him back the note which this time he folded neatly and slipped into his wallet.

"I guess Beverly must've straightened up my apartment," said McGovern. "I can't find a damn thing I'm looking for anymore."

"Same here," I said.

"By the way," said McGovern, "I'd appreciate it if you guys wouldn't mention any of this to Beverly. She tends to take a rather dim view of this sort of thing."

"I'll file it away with all your other secrets I've kept," said Myers. "Then one day I'll blackmail your ass for a bottle of twenty-five-year-old high-grade straight malt Macallan's scotch."

"And as for me," I said, "I've already consigned the entire episode to the precise location where it's always belonged."

"The Dikstuffer?" said Myers.

"No," I said. "The Theater for the Forgotten."

Chapter Forty-Eight

Several months passed and Polly Price was not heard from again. Possibly she'd vanished in the same mysterious way as her husband, whoever and wherever he was. With Polly's disappearance, there were other *desaparecidos* as well, though I don't believe McGovern consciously connected the two events. The Men in Black disappeared, along with the old Indian in the receding turban, the Gene Kelly impersonator on the fire escape, the little green man, and all the other phone calls, threats, and disturbances, real or imagined, that had plagued McGovern's world.

Even the winter seemed to have almost disappeared. Spring cannot always be considered spring in New York, but at least the streets and sidewalks and parks were no longer twelve inches deep in toxic, coffee-colored sludge, I was no longer freezing my balls off every time I got out of bed, and the cat, I noticed, was no longer hunkering down cowboy style beside the percolator.

It was a clear, crisp, beautiful Friday night in the city sometime around the middle of April and McGovern was having an intimate dinner party at his place which, I am not terribly shocked to report, was back to its usual state of comfortable disarray. McGovern's guest list that evening was limited to three: Beverly, Stephanie DuPont, and myself. The dish he was serving, which he'd labored all afternoon to prepare, was his famous, incomparable Chicken McGovern.

"That was the best chicken I've ever had in my life," said Stephanie, across the candlelight and chicken bones. "You've got to tell me how to make it."

"It's an Old World recipe," said McGovern. "It's rather complicated. For about thirty years I've kept it right up here." McGovern pointed to his very large and handsome head, but Stephanie, being young and impetuous, still wasn't satisfied.

"If it's not a secret," she said like a petulant child, "why can't I borrow it? Surely you've got the recipe written down somewhere."

"Stephanie," I said, "if McGovern doesn't want to give away his recipe he doesn't want to give away his recipe. You wouldn't dream of walking up to Colonel Sanders and asking him to give you his eleven different secret herbs and spices."

"First of all," said Stephanie, "I wouldn't be walking up to Colonel Sanders. He'd probably be crawling up to me and asking for my telephone number. Secondly, Mike McGovern can cook absolute circles around Colonel Sanders."

She favored McGovern with a stunning, admiring smile of such intensity that it could've launched a thousand cookbooks and floated them all the way to Troy. Basking in the afterglow, McGovern got up from the table and wandered into the kitchen, where he could be seen picking up a steak knife and prying loose a board under the sink. His three dinner guests looked on in mild amazement.

"There's a hidden compartment here," said McGovern, "where I keep my old recipes and stuff. I haven't opened it in years and I can't promise, but if I was a hard copy of Chicken McGovern, this is where I'd be."

"He's such an accommodating host," I clucked approvingly.

"I never knew that hidden compartment was there," said Beverly.

"That's what makes it a hidden compartment," said McGovern, as he extracted a sheaf of yellowed papers and proceeded to shake the dust and cobwebs off into the trash.

"He always ceases to amaze me," I said, as I lit an afterdinner cigar to the disapproving eye of Stephanie. But the main focus of the dinner guests was now clearly upon McGovern.

"Holy shit," he said, looking over the recipes.

"What?" I said.

"Now I remember where I got the recipe," said McGovern. "I memorized it so long ago that I'd forgotten. Leaning Jesus gave it to me."

"WHAT!" Stephanie and I shouted simultaneously.

Before Beverly could say "Who's Leaning Jesus?" the two of us were on our feet waiting as McGovern trundled the ancient document over to the table.

"Let me have a look," said Stephanie. "A girl knows about these things."

She gave McGovern another stunner of a smile and he put the recipe in her rapacious hands. I got up and put on my reading skepticals and walked around behind her as she sat back down to read the recipe. The ingredients and instructions were as follows:

The Marinade
three or four pound chicken cut up with back
    bone and wingtips used for stock
    fresh ginger
three scallions diced finely
drumsticks, thighs, and white meat scored,
    skinned, and cleaned of hidden fat pockets
two tsp roasted browned peppercorns
two TB soy sauce
sugar sprinkled to taste

The Sauce
four garlic cloves diced finely and mashed
four scallions diced finely
one stalk celery
a few stems fresh coriander or parsley
fresh grated ginger to taste
two TB light soy sauce
two tsp distilled white vinegar
four TB chicken stock
one TB tomato ketchup
sugar to taste
two TB sesame oil

You Also Require
cornstarch for dredging
nonfat oil for deep frying
toasted peanuts to taste

Putting It Together
Peel and grate the ginger finely.
Dice scallions into very fine rounds.
Divide chicken and put into bowl.
Score or prick with a sharp knife.
Sprinkle with ground peppercorns, ginger,
    scallions, soy sauce, and sugar.
Rub in well with hands.
Cover and refrigerate for four hours or
    overnight.

For the sauce, use two separate bowls.

In one bowl place the mashed garlic, diced
    scallions, and celery cut into very fine
    rounds.
Mash ginger and cut into minute dice.
Combine and set aside.
In the other bowl, stir well soy sauce, vinegar,
    stock, ketchup, sugar, and sesame oil.
Set aside.
After chicken is marinaded, set in a row and
    dust all over with cornstarch.
Pat chicken until mixture is well absorbed.
Set aside for twenty minutes.
Fry in hot vegetable oil until crusty.
Bake in oven at 350 degrees for thirty to forty
    minutes, dependent upon size of chicken
    pieces.
Drain on paper towel and place on serving
    dish.

Mix together the two bowls of sauce
    ingredients and bathe the chicken.
Sprinkle with toasted peanuts.
Open mouth.
Serve at once.

"Wait a minute," said Stephanie. "There's one more page to this."

"It's already the longest recipe in the world," I said.

It was also just about the most disappointing recipe in the world, I thought, as I poured myself a very generous portion of brandy and drifted over to the wall above the empty fireplace to share my sorrows with Carole Lombard. Sometimes, I reflected rather grimly, no matter who wrote it, who cooks it, who serves it, or who eats it, a recipe is just a recipe. Behind me, I supposed, Stephanie was still poring over the damn thing. I could hear McGovern describing to Beverly a rather humorous incident from the recent behavior of one rather notorious Mick Brennan. I downed an extremely large sip of brandy, gazed deeply into Lombard's eyes, and realized they bore an almost familial resemblance to Stephanie's.

Suddenly, either Lombard or Stephanie seemed to be speaking to me. Maybe it was both of them.

"Listen to this," the voice was saying. "'If you want to live dangerously (like I used to do), you might want to try.'"

"Try what?" said McGovern.

"Just some optional ingredients he lists here," said Stephanie.

"There *are* no optional ingredients to Chicken McGovern," said McGovern with some heat. "It's a very concise, very old family recipe."

"Hearts of palm," said Stephanie sweetly.

"No way," said McGovern.

"Between one and two large stone crabs sprinkled with sea salt?"

"Ridiculous."

"Just under one large tree-ripened tomato?"

"Insane!"

"Five deep-fried oysters?"

"Bullshit!"

"Simmer for ninety-five minutes?"

By this time McGovern was fairly well simmering himself. Beverly looked mildly amused. Stephanie appeared to be silently rereading the optional ingredients.

"Hearts of palm," I said. "That's Palm Island, Florida, where Al Capone died. He was known as the 'Master of 93 Palm Island,' his sprawling estate down there. Ninety-five minutes would be right next door. Drop a word or two out of each optional ingredient and I think we've got something."

"Got what?" asked Beverly.

"The secret to where Capone buried his treasure. A recipe's a perfect vehicle for a treasure map. It's the kind of thing you'd never think of in any other light than what it is. That's why McGovern didn't remember Leaning Jesus giving him anything."

"There's lots of other things I don't remember," said McGovern.

"That's why you're happy," I said.

But by now there were four happy people in the room. Five if you wanted to count Lombard. And I guess you might as well, because when I looked up at her eyes again I'd swear they were smiling.

Chapter Forty-Nine

"You see," I said to Stephanie as we walked home that night from McGovern's, "even the spiritual surveillance of all our lives doesn't infallibly turn up every mundane detail. Some little things always tend to slip between the cracks of our sidewalks and our souls."

A light rain was falling and, in the ancient glow of the streetlights, there seemed to form a canopy of hope and excitement over the city and the world. There were five and a half billion people and four hundred mountain gorillas left, I thought, and though I wasn't exactly sure which group I'd rather hang out with, I was finally beginning to have some fun at the party.

"What is old will be new," Stephanie was saying with a beatific expression on her beatific features. "What is lost will be found!"

"And what is tedious," I said, "is that Beverly won't let McGovern leave the city because of his recent disappearance. If we find the treasure we'll just give him his half."

"You mean his *third*," said Stephanie.

"You *are* going to make a good lawyer."

As we strolled through the crowded streets of the Village, Stephanie suddenly broke away, running ahead, then spinning around in sheer joy and exhilaration. And it must be reported that many a jaded Manhattanite looked on in a state of mass hypnosis as that remarkable girl jumped up and down, imbuing the stoic sidewalks of New York with a young and hopeful presence. Indeed, I, too, watched with a proud if somewhat prejudiced eye as she stood there shimmering in the grime, a cheerleader in the game of life.

"We're going to Disney World!" she shouted.

About the Author

Kinky Friedman lives in a little green trailer in a little green valley deep in the heart of Texas. There are about ten million imaginary horses in the valley and quite often they gallop around Kinky's trailer, encircling the author in a terrible, ever-tightening carousel of death. Even as the hooves are pounding around him in the darkest night, one can hear, almost in counterpoint, the frail, consumptive, ascetic novelist tip-tip-tapping away on the last typewriter in Texas. In such fashion he has turned out nine novels including *God Bless John Wayne*, *Armadillos & Old Lace*, and *Elvis, Jesus & Coca-Cola*. Two cats, Dr. Scat and Lady Argyle; a pet armadillo called Dilly; and a small black dog named Mr. Magoo can sometimes be found sleeping with Kinky in his narrow, monastic, Father Damien-like bed.

IF YOU HAVE ENJOYED READING THIS
LARGE PRINT BOOK AND YOU WOULD
LIKE MORE INFORMATION ON HOW TO
ORDER A WHEELER LARGE PRINT
BOOK, PLEASE WRITE TO:

WHEELER PUBLISHING, INC.
P. O. BOX 531
ACCORD, MA 02018-0531

A·B
3-4-98

X